Hounds of Heaven

Another Tale Of The Blue Panda

Tree of Life Publishing

A CIP catalogue record for this book is available from the British Library.

ISBN: 978-1-915816-01-6

Tree of Life Publishing
Devon, UK

Hounds of Heaven

Another Tale Of The Blue Panda

Maggy Whitehouse

In loving memory of Destiny-Decibel Biggle Wiggle

Other fiction by Maggy Whitehouse

The Book Of Deborah (Tree of Life Publishing)
Into the Kingdom (Tree of Life Publishing)
Leaves of the Tree (Tree of Life Publishing)
The Miracle Man (O Books)
For The Love Of Dog (Tree of Life Publishing)
Tales Of The Blue Panda (Tree of Life Publishing)

Chapter One

I THINK I'M falling in love with a ghost.

Technically, he isn't a ghost because we met in the afterlife and, over there, I'm the one who tends to be pale and slightly transparent although, unfortunately, not ethereally thin. At least, in the heavens, we don't have to worry about the age difference, given that he is approximately twelve hundred years older than I am.

Marcus is not in love with me because he has what we living folk would call a brain and the dead folk call "sense". However, we do hang out sometimes and, given that the afterlife is ineffable, sometimes we manage to drink tea and eat chocolate biscuits together. Although that's only if I bring them. Nowadays we laugh a lot but we weren't laughing when we met.

It began at Christmas. Not *all* vicars secretly hate Christmas but quite a lot of us do. More accurately, it's more exasperation and exhaustion with snippy bits. We ache for Boxing Day when we can get seriously drunk, forget the stupidities and calamities of the weeks beforehand and get back to the real Work (which is not the getting drunk part, honest).

Why? Well, let's start with the nativity play and that very wise saying of "never work with children or animals". There was the year when the baby Jesus was eaten by the donkey. To be fair, the baby was a rag doll stuffed with hay and therefore rather tempting but it didn't look good on the day. Then there was the year when the baby Jesus was dropped into the generous gift that the donkey had already donated on the church floor; not to mention the year that the baby Jesus was part of a tug-of-war between Mary and Joseph over who got to cuddle him and Mary pulled his head off. Or the year that the baby Jesus was a real baby (and the donkey was *very* tightly tethered) and we sang about the poor baby in the manger while he dozed in a high-tech baby stroller which would have cost all the gold, frankincense and myrrh and then some.

Everyone wants a live donkey in the Nativity and we get one from the local sanctuary… but nobody seems to clock the fact that Mary is supposed to be riding *on* it because she's too pregnant to walk. Our Marys usually lead the donkey and it doesn't even carry any luggage. It really is the most pointless sort of donkey ever, apart from the part which is useful for my roses. The one time I persuaded Mary actually to ride the donkey, she fell off. She wasn't hurt but the landing caused the realistic bump under her tunic to fall out which meant that, innovatively, Jesus was born *on the way* to Bethlehem that year.

Then there's the crib in the church. I'm Anglo-Indian so I tend to object to the whiter-than-white baby Jesus with the ghastly orange hair rather more than my equally whiter-than-white parishioners do. I did once suggest re-painting him in more Middle Eastern colours but that was about as popular as a real vicar at a tarts and vicars fancy dress party… But it's the *size* of the baby that's the main issue, for me. It's as big as an eight-year-old. You may not believe in any of the Christmas stories of virgin births, wise men or the star of Bethlehem but anyone, *anyone* must consider it a miracle that a fourteen-year-old girl could give birth to a baby that size without exploding.

People come to church at Christmas because it has a huge tree with pretty lights and carols that they know and it's 'traditional.' Yes, it's nice to have the building stuffed to the rafters, for once, but if you're going to come at Christmas, *please* do explain some of what's going on to your children beforehand. Far too many parents tell their six or seven-year-old at Midnight Mass that there will be a lovely surprise at the end of the service—and what would a little child expect at Midnight on Christmas Eve? Father Christmas, of course. Instead, their parents take them to see a plaster baby with orange hair who has miraculously arrived in the manger, courtesy of my assistant, Lucie (and rather a lot of glue given that the donkey trod on it last year). The over-tired, bored and confused children look at it in horror, open their mouths, yell, 'Why's Santa got no clothes on?' and the police really don't need the hassle. They have to come *every time* because safeguarding is a major issue but Inspector Marks and her team are usually very stoical about it. Nowadays, we've got quite a routine of at least three police officers in my kitchen for a mug of Horlicks and a slice of Christmas cake at two o'clock on Christmas morning. I'm beginning to wonder if I should bake a bigger cake.

This particular Christmas was the one when the ghost dog arrived. I don't think I've ever had a dog though I've got nothing against them. If that sentence sounds weird, I don't *know* if I've ever had a dog because about fifteen years of my life is missing after what was probably a car accident following a murder attempt by another vicar who was possessed by a demon. Head injuries are life changing and my life was transformed to the extent that I actually have some justification for forgetting what day it is and falling in love with ghosts. It's always possible, though unlikely, that a dog of some kind was involved somewhere along the way. Considerable patches of memory have come back but, apparently, I may never recover the rest. The perpetrator of the situation didn't come back at all so we can't clarify what happened there either. All I know for sure is that I woke up with a hole in my head and the ability to travel between the worlds which, I suppose, is a reasonably fair exchange for losing a load of memories that, in retrospect, were mostly less than useful. Without memory it's *far* easier to forgive people because you can't work out what it was that what they did, or didn't do, that offended you in the first place. Take my ex-husband for example: he lives in my parish and, from simple observation, I have deduced that he's a bit of a prat but, as I have sod-all recall about our life together, there's nothing I can actually blame him for and I really rather like his new wife. He appears to find that rather surprising. What I do find constantly amazing is why I would have wanted to marry him in the first place.

Oh, and before I forget… most nights, since the accident/murder attempt, I am driven off to the afterlife by my dead brother, Jon, in his 1990s blue Fiat Panda. It seems so normal to me now that it's almost an afterthought to mention it.

I suppose Jon is also a ghost but, it seems to me after nearly a year of this way of life, that the healthy dead are far more vibrant than most of the living. The unhealthy dead are another matter… They are my part-time job and the full-time work of my other dead friends, Sam and Callista.

When I'm with Jon, we can operate outside of space and time which means that, after a week or so away, I get home about a minute after I left. Apparently, it's quantum. In Kairos time, I must be about sixty by now though on Earth, in Chronos time, I'm forty-four.

I see angels too, by the way, just so you're fully in the picture. And no, I don't discuss all this with relevant archdeacons, deans or (nowadays) bishops.

Of course, there is the possibility that I'm making all this up because have a head injury and I ought to see a(nother) psychiatrist, or even go for voluntary admission in some place where they medicate you out of your delusions, but I'm happy, I get to hang out with Jon and souls get saved so where's the harm? And I'm a vicar, so it's my job. We are *meant* to save souls; all of 'em, not just the ones that signed up to our particular party, whatever the fundamentalists say.

There's a rumour that there are neighbourhoods in the heavens where people who had strong religious beliefs live in a kind of conclave that locks out anyone different so that they don't have to face the fact that the afterlife doesn't give a rap what you believed in or even who you were. Everyone is welcome. So far, I haven't seen any evidence of such neighbourhoods but anything is possible.

That particular Christmas night, I finally stopped binge-watching *The West Wing* and went to bed. One of the best things about memory loss is that you can re-view box sets of shows you have completely forgotten but can love all over again. That only works if you've still got the DVDs of course; you'll probably have no idea what you might have streamed or recorded and deleted.

I was cleaning my teeth while standing on one leg. Balance issues are a common side-effect of a head injury and teaching myself to stand on one leg as often as possible is a way to retrain my brain by making it work on the issue directly.

Something touched my left calf. That was the one with a foot on the floor. It took a moment to realise that this wasn't the belt of my towelling dressing gown and it took another moment to realise that the action was being repeated up and down the leg. Something was touching me on purpose.

Something invisible.

Now, I do understand that the normal reaction to such an experience would be to go 'bleugh!' and start flapping towels around but I do hope you realise by now that I am not normal. I was slightly annoyed rather than frightened. Given my life-choices it was almost certainly some kind of ghost and I really, *really* wanted a night off. Jon had promised to give me a whole three-day break from Christmas night to the day after Boxing Day. I was supposed to have had Christmas Eve off, too, but there had been a small cosmic crisis with a dead film star being prevented from crossing over safely due to the anguished grief of his fans calling him back which meant that I had done seven hours extra in two minutes somewhere around three AM, after the police had left, stuffed with Horlicks and cake.

Cautiously, I put the other foot down on the floor. There was a pause and then the ghost began the touching again, this time on the fresh leg. I stood there probably for a full five minutes—which is a lot longer than you think it is—until it stopped. By then, I had deduced that the action was something licking me rather than touching so it was some kind of animal. Nothing else happened which was good, indicating that the licking wasn't being undertaken as an aperitif. This appeared to be a short, friendly ghost that liked drying wet legs. Or, as previously stated, it could be a delusion caused by a head injury.

To be honest, I forgot about it because nothing else unusual happened that night. I spent Boxing Day in glorious seclusion, tramping over Dartmoor, scoffing myself silly and revering the genius of Aaron Sorkin.

After my bath that night, the same thing happened. Something dried my feet and my legs and then moved away. And the next night too. I spoke to it, gently, bidding it welcome—on the hopeful assumption that it might understand me and, that third night, I could have sworn that, just before I dropped off to sleep, there was a subtle pressure by my feet in the bed as if something had jumped up and settled down. I sat up to look but there was nothing to see.

On 28th December, when Jon came to pick me up, I asked him what he thought. It was a fairly routine trip that night; just ensuring that a couple of atheists found their way through. They, understandably, thought they weren't dead but had gone mad or invisible or something. It's not my job to explain the heavens to them—there are whole ranges of experts in the spirit world for that. Generally, atheists are brilliant to deal with because they are surprised and delighted to find that there *is* an afterlife after all and that no one gives a rap what you believed on Earth. We are warned on pain of being born again never, *ever* to say 'I told you so.'

'Do you think it's a dog?' I asked. 'Whatever it is, it must be around for a reason. I can't see it—the beast, or the reason.'

'Dunno,' said Jon, swerving to avoid an asteroid. I should explain that each night we take a ridiculous, symbolic and highly enjoyable trip through the Universe in the blue Panda to get to and from the afterlife. It isn't necessary for more advanced souls but, as had been carefully and tactfully revealed to me, living people need to pass through a filtering process to be able to access the realms of the dead. We are thick energies whereas the higher realms are finer ones. We live in what feels like murky water to them but beyond the stars it is all light. I can't access vast areas of the afterlife for two reasons: 1. I'm not dead and 2. I am too dense a vibration not to burn out. That changes after you die—at least it does if you get through. And if you don't, well, there are people like me and Jon and Sam and Callista all over the Universe to bring you safely home.

'We could ask Marcus if he's missing anyone,' said Jon.

'Marcus? Anyone?'

'Marcus is the Dog Wrangler. He receives all the domestic dogs that die so they know they are coming home. I think he must be one third human, one third angel and one third dog.'

'What?'

Jon sighed. 'Okay... well as far as I know, animals belong to a group soul but because so many of them have individuated so much through being pets, dogs, especially, need someone they love and recognise to greet them when they die. It takes them a while to adapt back into the group where they can be a hundred percent soul-dog again. Marcus takes them through birth and welcomes them back at death so they already know and love him.'

'What, *all* of them?'

'That I don't know; probably he's part of a team like we are. But he's the only Dog Wrangler I've met so I think we'd better go and see him about your ghost hound tonight. You'll need to hold my hand and not let go. Oh, and you'll need a hanky...'

The couple were very quiet in the vet's waiting room. At their feet sat an old dog, her fur dusty with grey hairs and her eyes cloudy. They, loving her as they did, could not bear to see her suffer any more and had made the kindest but most painful decision. Other people waiting with their pets cast sympathetic looks; all could tell by the expressions on the couple's faces, and the way they fondled their beloved's ears, that this was the last hour of the little dog's life.

It felt incredibly intrusive to go into the vet's room with them but Jon was insistent. 'You need to see this,' he said. 'Every human being who has ever loved a pet needs to see this. And, in any case, it's the only way I know of that we can get through to that particular dimension.'

We stood, invisible in the corner—and don't ask me 'how?' because I don't know and I didn't care—while the vet, as kindly as she could, talked the couple through the procedure and put the catheter in the little mongrel's leg. Bracken tried to pull her paw away, not knowing what was happening or why.

The woman who had loved Bracken so deeply for thirteen years held her and spoke her name gently, praising her and telling her what a wonderful friend she had been, while her partner, also with tears in his eyes, stood beside her... and the vet put the little dog to sleep.

Two scenarios played out instantly; firstly, the palpable grief of the couple as the dog's body slumped in the woman's arms. And, from a different dimension, a being of light was also there, filling all the spaces in the living woman's cells, so that he was the first thing the spirit of the dog would sense as she passed through the veil.

Bracken lifted her spirit head, her eyes re-focused, her nose twitched and she gave a yelp of excitement. And then this tired old dog, transformed, leapt into the Being's arms, crying with joy at being reunited with a love as great as that she had known on Earth.

And the Being loved her too. His arms wrapped around her, he held her until he realised that she was well and began to jump and run around the room in delight. The Being ran too as the little mongrel chased him and jumped up at him, eyes bright, tongue out and voice uttering cries of excitement. She didn't look back once as they ran through the different-dimension open door together and they both vanished into the ether.

Bodies work differently in the spirit world but I still couldn't see for tears as Jon took my hand and pulled me through that door into the Dimension of Animal Souls.

Chapter Two

Now I have to try and explain the inexplicable. Bear with me, please, because that's going to happen a lot. Throughout the following experience I asked 'But how? How? How?' and every time I was answered but every time the answer was beyond my comprehension. You know those situations when someone is patiently explaining something that is beyond the stratosphere of your brain's ability to comprehend? Usually it's not because you're thick; it's because you can't begin from the same starting point that they have. This time, I didn't even know where that starting point was, let alone how to find it.

I suppose the easiest thing to say might be that the *whole* of the heavens is about re-membering what we humans so love to dis-remember and dismember. We have taught and learnt that God is only loving if you obey certain rules; that humans are more valuable than any other species; that only humans have souls and so many other limitations and laws that are, basically, the way that we try to control God. The human race couldn't handle an all-loving, all-forgiving God because we work transactionally, not transformationally. We require justice which is usually our word for revenge. If the phrase 'if you behave, I will love you,' is at all familiar then you will have a fine, inbuilt concept of what I call "kindergarten religion."

Most vicars, frankly, still teach this but I think it's time for us to grow up. And, as you can probably understand from the preceding rant, I'm not entirely popular within the Church of England, let alone with the odd bishop. My diocese has a new bishop; the last one ended up getting murdered while investigating demonic possession in a paedophile ring. As you do… He was a good egg; I only found out I'd been in love with him after he died — memory loss is a bastard sometimes. He was in love with me too, by the way; in fact we were engaged. I can now, vaguely, remember loving him and I still have the ring but nearly all the other details escape me. I have no recall at all of our time as lovers, of how he (or I?) proposed or what our plans might have been.

We'll get back to the new bishop later because you are, understandably, far more interested in Bracken and Marcus.

Jon and I found ourselves in a place that exuded the great soul of Dog. The oversoul is the receptacle of all kinds of dogs from wolves to Chihuahuas and within it rest more specific types. It was profoundly and gloriously smelly! The wild part of this great soul seemed to be a festival of joyous hunting and sleeping; the highly-bred-by-humans part, a great cradle of love. I could perceive spirit dogs moving back and forth between the different essences, in a kind of ripple effect, and overall there was a feeling of a great mother dog, watching over her puppies.

It was a grand place with great, wide, flowing vistas for fun and, for the first time ever, I could understand something of what sight and scent means to the canine brain. Extraordinary, differing smells flowed through a multitude of colours I could taste and the images were both subtler and far clearer than my human sight is used to. I knew that if I could only perceive like this on Earth, I would never misplace my trust again.

Bracken was playing with a man in what looked like a park on the outskirts of the great soul. The man was throwing a ball for her and she raced back and forwards, tongue hanging out, her spirit body suffused with delight. I found myself watching man more than dog, appreciating his wholehearted engagement with the little creature, how he spoke to her and his expressions as he laughed and praised her. Bracken's tail wagged nineteen-to-the-dozen.

'That's Marcus,' said Jon.

Marcus presented as a fully-mature man; darker skinned than me, so probably half-blood African heritage, with kinky-curly hair and he was—frankly—gorgeous. I found myself idly wondering whether five-o'clock shadow was a heavenly style choice or if discarnate souls still needed razors. His clothing was that of someone used to living in hot climates: a tunic with a belt and sandals. This was not a young soul. Oh, and great legs too…

I don't know if Jon and I were invisible or how long passed in terms of Earthly time but, somehow, we were able to watch what I would call years-within-years passing outside of time. For what seemed like weeks, Bracken stayed close to Marcus, learning easily to adapt to dozens of other dogs who came through to this land and slowly but steadily becoming more interested in and involved with the other spirit dogs—mostly those similar to her. She would merge into the great soul happily whenever Marcus went away on another mission and greet him enthusiastically on his return. Eventually, Bracken found that she preferred staying in the soul with the other dogs and so she herself began to merge.

At this point Jon, who was still holding my hand, made a little movement in what—for convenience's sake—I will call "the air" and the loose apparatus I would normally call "time" shifted more. I saw Bracken's owner—the woman—appear in this wonderful land, brought by the column of light that was her guardian angel. She looked older than when I'd seen her on Earth but not *old*.

'Did you move us through time? Is she dead?' I whispered to Jon. He squeezed my hand.

'Sort of. There *isn't* any time here; it's all *now*. But I moved it so you could perceive a linear effect.'

Wow. Not to mention, WTAF?

The woman and her guardian angel approached Marcus and I could see the hope on her face.

He took a strand of energy from her (I can't explain it better than that) and—this was surprisingly shocking—walked *into* the group soul itself. I found that if I focused my attention, no matter how deep he went, I could still perceive him within this flowing, steaming, stinky, gorgeous energy field, offering the strand of energy as a kind of call. Somehow, I could make out a small stream of energy, pooling into a form beside him as Bracken individuated out of the whole. Marcus stroked her as she woke into recognition again and licked Marcus's hand.

He brought Bracken out of the soul and I needed my spirit hanky as the woman and her dog greeted each other again after—how many Earth years? And yet simultaneously I knew that, to the dog, hardly a moment had passed since the two had been together before.

'She can keep Bracken with her for all of her time here... and she can bring her back to the Soul if she has other things to do that mean the dog would be alone,' whispered Jon. 'Bracken loves and remembers the group Soul so she is content either way. This is what happens to all pets so they don't miss their humans and they remember how to love them the moment they see them again.'

'What if you've had more than one pet and love them all?'

'Then you can have all of them at once or one at a time. I expect there's even a way of merging them all into one happy spirit animal, if that's the best way for everyone, but that kind of energy blending is way beyond my pay grade.'

'That's perfect,' I gulped.

'That's heaven,' said Jon.

'And it's the same with all pets?'

'Well, it's funnier in the cat heaven because most of them don't give a rat's arse but they do appreciate their human pets returning so they can ignore them again.'

I snorted with laughter. The sound caught Marcus's attention. As Bracken and her human left the dimension, he turned towards us. Both Jon and he made the same small movement in the air that transported time and, somehow, I knew we were back in what I can only call contemporary spirit time according to my physical life.

'Greetings,' said Marcus, prosaically, as if he hadn't just been instrumental in more miracles than I could count. 'What can I do for you good folk?'

His voice was pleasantly gravelly and his accent was slightly old English which I found fascinating, given his colour. His dark brown eyes smiled as deeply as his mouth and I felt that old, familiar frisson that meant a small but significant chemical reaction was taking place in the brain that I currently, technically, didn't have.

Jon introduced us.

'This is Bella, Marcus. She's my sister. She's not dead so I can't let go of her hand.'

Marcus raised his eyebrows. 'A Soul Restorer? As I live and breathe! Which of course, I don't but even so... I haven't met one of you before. Good day!'

'Hello! I've never met a Dog Wrangler. How do you do?'

He laughed. 'I do very well, I thank you. What do you need of me?'

'Erm… Well, something has started licking my leg at night while I'm cleaning my teeth. I think it's a spirit dog but I can't see it. And I don't know what to do.'

'Hmmm.' He thought for a moment. 'It's not often that we miss a death of a human-bonded dog. That's certainly unusual. Sometimes they do choose to stay for a while if they were *very* emotionally tied to the human. Did you ever have a dog of your own?'

'No. Never. As far as I know, that is… I lost some of my memory.'

'Hmm. Jon, did Bella ever have a dog?'

'No.'

'All right, then I suspect it's a hound from your local hunt pack. You have hunting near where you live?'

'Drag hunting, yes.'

'Then almost certainly a hound. A pack is attached to humans but not the way that pets are so they generally go straight through to the group soul of Hound very happily. Looks like this one missed the call somehow. Shall I come and collect her?'

'Yes please. Her?'

'Yes. I'm starting to pick up her force-field now that I'm talking to you. She has imprinted on you enough for me to reach her.'

He paused, as if listening. I noticed that the more we spoke with him, the less archaic his accent and words. If he'd been software, I'd have thought he was updating himself.

'Yes. She died three weeks after having puppies—her second litter—so she stayed initially for them. But they've grown up and she seems to have some other reason for staying. I'm not sure what but I'm glad she found you.' He smiled at me and it felt as if the sun came out after a decade of fog.

'Why would she lick my legs?'

'Hounds usually clean themselves after a run; they don't get towelled down like pets do so they have to check themselves over and dry themselves. And she's a mother dog so she would have cleaned both herself and her puppies. She's trying to bond with you.'

'But why me?'

'Possibly she's able to perceive that you are in contact with the dead and might be able to help her?'

'Ah. Yes. Um.'

'Do you want to come with us, Marcus?' asked Jon. 'Bella has a spiritual algorithm that means we drive my old car back and forth through the solar system and the Universe. It's fun.'

'Gramercy!' said Marcus, thereby indicating that he'd certainly lived a life on Earth a good six hundred years ago. It's a sort of medieval 'Good grief, yes. Thanks!' based on the French 'grande merci.' I hadn't mentioned that I used to be an archaeologist or expert in ancient languages, had I? Weilway…

To add to that extraordinary night, we had the fun of experiencing Marcus's first ever journey in a car. Obviously, once he'd got over the speed and the claustrophobia and the views, he assumed that all cars travelled at light-speed across Universes because why would you not? He'd heard about the planets and seen a couple in the sky but, having been somewhat heavenly since his last death, from cholera, in 1853, he'd never even seen a photograph.

We arrived back outside my lovely old stone house in the village of Tayford in Devon and Jon parked on the verge which, strictly speaking, wasn't necessary as any passing car could just drive right through the blue Panda; but old habits die hard.

'Beautiful,' said Marcus, looking at the hoar frost on the hawthorn and wild rose hedge in front of the house. It is beautiful. I live in an earthly heaven on Dartmoor. Every morning, when I draw my curtains, the moor rises up before me in a magical landscape of heather purple, gorse gold and the palest of greens.

'She's upstairs,' said Marcus and, cheerfully walking *through* my white picket gate and the old, dark oak front door, he led the way.

Jon can do the same but I've learnt at my peril that it's painful to knees and heads to even attempt it so I opened both gate and door to follow.

The ghost hound was curled up on my bed and, with Marcus

there, I could see her. She was a foxhound, creamy in colour rather than patchy (is that the right word?) and she thumped the end of her tail in a slightly embarrassed manner when she saw us, as if to say 'am I allowed on here?'

Marcus spoke to her in Hound. No, I don't know how. I'd been 'how?ing'—as opposed to 'howling'—in the car all the way home and I still didn't have a clue.

She rolled over on her back so that he could tickle her ghostly tummy and talked back. It wasn't 'talking' but it was communicating. He listened.

'Very well,' he said, in human, and gave her a pat which obviously meant 'I'm stopping the tickling now.' She sat up and looked at me.

'She isn't coming back with me,' said Marcus. 'At least not yet. She says she's to stay with you.'

'Me?'

'Yes, she wants to protect you.'

'Protect me? From what?'

'Rus-El and Hero say you need each other.'

I wouldn't go as far as to say I *know* Hero but I know she's there. She's my guardian angel. But Rus-El?

'Rus-El was destroyed,' I said, stupidly, as if he would understand. 'He was my angel of protection but he was annihilated.'

Marcus seemed to listen for a minute. 'No…' he said. '*A* Rus-El was destroyed but he was an angel and all angels are one-offs—spin-offs from their Archangel, if you like. New angels are always being created from the Source of that Archangel and Rus-El is a new creation with the same name. He is to become your protector but for the moment it's this hound.'

'Oh no…' I shook my head. 'Please don't tell me I'm going to need more protection!'

Marcus smiled in a way that gave me collywobbles. 'I'll come back when she's ready to leave,' he said and simply faded away into the ether.

'Marcus?' I said, foolishly, to try and hold onto him. It didn't work. Just Jon and I were standing in the bedroom with a ghost hound. My heart plummeted to realise that Jon could also just vanish in the same way, one day. I lost him once, so long ago, and I could so easily lose him again. Spontaneously, I threw my arms around him and, to the surprise of us both, I began to cry.

I don't often cry; not because I'm tough or because I'm embarrassed but because I cry stupendously beautifully and, oddly, any sob that comes out sounds like laughter. That can cause a lot of misunderstandings. Of course, refusing to cry makes you look tough but that's better than looking beautifully insensitive. I can and do cry with Jon because I feel safe enough to do so.

'Tea!' I said, pulling myself together.

'And chocolate biscuits?' said Jon hopefully. It's an odd thing about dead folk; well, there are lots of odd things about dead folk… but it seems that they still like to have tea or coffee and treats with the living, given half the opportunity. And apparently, they can only do it *with* a member of the living. I've often thought those TV shows that look for ghosts would be a lot more successful if they used Choco Leibniz as bait.

Another odd thing about dead folk is that they seem fully corporeal to me when I'm with them. We can hug, for example. I can't tell you how good it is to be able to hug someone after a break of more than twenty years.

I could still just about see the hound and she seemed quite happy to stay curled up on my bed, so we trailed downstairs to my lovely farmhouse kitchen with its old wooden table, the Aga, the kettle, the tea caddy and the big tin of biscuits.

Jon died when I was eighteen, by the way and, until then, he was all the mother and father I had known from the age of six when our parents were killed in a car crash. He taught me my love of history, archaeology and questioning everything. Kind of ironic given that we have ended up in a universe where, even if he could explain how things work, I couldn't possibly comprehend.

'Was there something specific we were supposed to do tonight?' I asked him as I got the milk out of the fridge.

'Yes, but we can do it tomorrow,' said Jon, taking a third chocolate-covered shortbread. 'These are *gooood!*'

'The world of biscuits has come a long way since your time,' I said, sitting down. 'I remember, coming home from Iraq and

China with you and being horrified at the range and opulence of the food in our shops. It seemed totally over the top. Now it's a thousand times worse—or better, depending on your point of view.'

'And the Middle East has been corrupted by chocolate biscuits too,' said Jon.

'You think that's the problem?'

He laughed. 'Hardly, but it all contributes, doesn't it? One half of the world wants what the other half has and demands more for itself.'

Dear God, never let me forget to give thanks that I get to sit and talk thus with my brother who has been dead for more than a quarter of a century. Whatever happens in my life, I know that I am blessed.

Famous last words, eh?

Chapter Three

Monday is my day off so I try to treat myself to a lie-in and, occasionally, I even get a cup of tea in bed. No, that's not true: I *always* have a cup of tea in bed because I have a teasmade with a teapot that is dark brown with tannin inside and makes the best cuppa in the world. But on some Mondays, Mrs Teague brings me up a mug of tea if only to give her an excuse to nag me about something.

Mrs Teague, better known as "Mrs Tiggy" for her resemblance to Beatrix Potter's *Mrs Tiggywinkle,* is the archetypical stroppy housekeeper with a heart of gold wrapped in a vinegar-soaked lemon. Every vicar should have one and, of course, every fictional vicar does. My own personal archetype is also my part-time PA. I swear, in a previous life she must have been a doctor's receptionist because it's harder to get past Mrs Tiggy than it would be to sneak by Cerberus at the entrance to Hades. She's happy to be called Mrs Tiggy but you must never forget the "Mrs" because it's about respect. Obviously. Once Mrs Tiggy asked me, all aspects bristling, whether I regarded her as a servant. Luckily, my hastily-formulated, '*No!* As a valued assistant!' cut the mustard.

Mrs Tiggy is my armour, my greatest support, my strongest critic and she thinks I'm hopelessly weird even without having a clue what I get up to at night. I once, foolishly, told her that I believed in angels but, apparently, while they were perfectly acceptable back in Biblical days, we don't have any now. It's the same with miracles; they happened in Biblical times but not in the modern day. I suppose God just gave up on us somewhere along the line and couldn't be arsed? Sometimes I tell Mrs Tiggy that my life has been a series of miracles and her presence in my life is one of them, even if only to hear her fabulous '*Pshw!*' that,

I swear, makes all the crockery in the kitchen sit up straighter and the biscuits re-arrange themselves neatly in the tin.

This day, she brought both tea and reinforcements. But not good ones.

I don't have a *problem* with children; in fact, I find them very useful barometers for my sanity. Tell a child what's on the day's news and he or she will generally come up with a very succinct comment, such as, 'Any dragons today? Any dinosaurs? I've got new socks,' which, to me, puts the ridiculousness of the world's politics safely back in its box.

But there are children and children… and there are Mrs Tiggy's grandchildren who quite frequently turn up with her during school holidays. She takes care of them while their parents are at work.

Oliver and Iris are twins. I think they are nine; I've been told often enough but I don't pay attention, probably because they're not dragons or dinosaurs. I'd rather have dragons; in the worst-case scenario you could rebuild your house with the insurance (we vicars agree that dragon flamings do not constitute an "act of God") or, at least, avoid having to pay for your own cremation. And when dragons break or flame things, you know straight away; you don't discover the damage several weeks later. Oliver and Iris break little things like pencils, flowers, mugs, ornaments and old lockets inherited from your dead mother and, consequently, hearts.

Even Mrs Tiggy, who would defend her darlings to the hilt, did pause when I showed her how Iris had painted over my parents' fading faces with green felt pen and broken the locket's old bobbly rose gold chain which had belonged to my great-grandmother.

'Well, it's not as if you wear it, Bella!' she said, eventually pulling herself back on track. 'And you can replace the pictures. I'm sure she didn't mean to upset you.'

I couldn't replace the pictures and I think she did. They're building anti-theists younger and younger nowadays and both Oliver and Iris think I'm a boring old anachronism and that my beautiful Norman church, St. Raphael's, is a waste of space. They think it's funny that I'm supposed to be "good" and like to try and push my buttons to prove that I'm not. This, of course, would not be a problem if I didn't have buttons to push…

It's not that I have an issue with atheists, by the way; some of my best friends and all that… Actually, that's not quite true, my best friend is a Pagan which, within the Christian community, is frequently regarded as a great deal worse. In fact, I think genuine atheists are usually better Christians in action than most folk who have signed on the official dotted line—not to mention less hypocritical—but atheistic cynics and anti-theists annoy me with their laziness. They look at conventional religion and reject it all on appearance without looking any deeper. A lot of faiths do end up being part of the system focusing on the letter of the law, not its spirit, and losing all the magic (and then complaining that you're using a word like "magic"), but it's often the classic situation of judging a book by its cover. Anti-theists are hardly different from fundamentalists in living in the cast-iron certainty that they are right and plying contempt along with their conviction. Certainty is the *opposite* of faith and the foundation of prejudice. But I think even anti-theists who damage much-loved heirlooms are better than religious fundamentalists who force-feed the dirty bath water, having long thrown out the holy baby.

But I digress… in a nutshell, I don't like Mrs Tiggy's grandchildren and they don't like me. I pretend that I do like them because death-by-cutting-comments is Mrs Tiggy's modus operandi at the best of times (my colleague Robbie calls it *Scalding-Scolding*) and most days I simply tune out the first five minutes of her speech. Once I did mutter, 'Scold!' She heard me and my heart plummeted until she replied, 'yes, it is for the time of year…' and suggested I put on a cardy.

This particular Monday morning, the unholy Trinity arrived in my bedroom complete with a mug of tea, the post and Oliver's accurate but unnecessary comment that I looked like shit, followed by Mrs Tiggy's routine Scalding-Scolding about swearing.

'*No!*' I said as Iris gravitated over towards my ancient and battle-scarred dressing table to search for pretty things to play with. I suppose vicars—particularly middle-aged vicars—

shouldn't possess such things as sexy underwear and, if they do, should also expect nine-year-olds to wear them on their heads like frilly headphones while playing action heroes in the garden, at the exact moment that the Parish Council arrives.

So far, so normal and only averagely irritating. But something else was not so normal; I had a ghost hound. I'd forgotten all about her and she was certainly invisible again but I could hear something; not in my ears but through my throat… she was growling.

That in itself didn't disturb me so much; I feel like growling when uninvited children barge into my bedroom before I am dressed. But when a ghost hound jumps under the bed to hide and begins to bark, something might just be up.

The barking, by the way, was like a repeating echo; a jangly soft cacophony of vibrations. I put my hand down the side of the bed and felt a ghostly nose touch it. I don't know who was reassuring whom but I think we both felt a little better.

Iris stopped on my command and turned, instead, to the chest of drawers on which stood a little leather-bound box of coloured stones, shards and shells that I had collected (mostly legally) from all over the world in the days when I was an archaeologist. This, on previous occasions, had been emptied all over the floor to be browsed through before being left for me to tread on the contents with bare feet.

'These are *so* pretty, Auntie Bella,' she said, running her fingers through the bright treasures, surprisingly still all inside their container. 'I love your box of bones.'

For a moment, I considered denying that it was a box of bones but stones are the bones of the Earth, after all, and I thought that it would be better to respond encouragingly to a positive comment. 'My favourite is the lapis,' I said (foolish, *foolish* Bel!). 'That beautiful deep blue stone.'

'This one?' Iris held up a smooth, tumbled piece of blue glass the size of a thumbnail and, before I could say, 'no, not that,' had put it into her mouth and swallowed it. At that exact moment, something else looked at me out of her eyes.

The next half hour was tied up with recriminations and calling *NHS Direct* who said it should be perfectly fine and, simultaneously, that it might not be. Iris demonstrated that nothing had stuck in her trachea by happily scoffing several biscuits from my kitchen cookie jar while her grandmother was on the phone in the hall, so it was increasingly likely that the foreign object would go through safely, but the nice lady at *NHS Direct* was emphatic that we should call an ambulance if Iris got any symptoms of discomfort.

I knew she wouldn't; my deeply-suspicious soul could tell that whatever it was that had looked out of her eyes, and that prompted her to eat something she believed I loved, was certainly going to look forward to the idea of my having to examine her poo to retrieve it. Luckily, the blue glass had no sentimental value so I, heartlessly, told Iris to watch out for a "clunk" in the lavatory and do whatever she wanted with the result.

'Don't you want it back, Auntie Bella?' she asked, all wide-eyed innocence.

'Not after it's been through you!' snorted her brother.

'No, thank you,' I said, sweetly. 'It was just a sea-tumbled stone from Bude.'

Yes, there it was again; the quick shutter opening in the eyes while Iris herself pouted with disappointment. Trust me on this; I'm a trained and practising exorcist and I know possession when it shows its often strangely-enticing face. But there are rules in exorcism; you can *only* do it when there's at least two of you to do the work or you could be seriously outnumbered… and if the human is perfectly happy to host the demonic, you may do far more harm than good. Apart from those (and several other) rules, carrying out an exorcism on a child can be a bit of a problem within the terms of safeguarding…

There are exceptions—as there are with any law—such as when a life is being directly threatened but this wasn't one of them. This was a watching brief.

By the end of the morning, I knew for sure and I also knew that whatever it was had both of the twins in its thrall. If I hadn't been on high alert I wouldn't have been able to catch Oliver's hand in time when he caught hold of one of my fingers, trying to bend it backwards.

'*Ow!* You *hurt* me!' he yelled, even though I certainly hadn't.

It was just one of those days for your average exorcist time-and-space-travelling rural vicar.

I hid the lapis—in fact the whole box—somewhere where even they couldn't find it.

When they had all gone, around lunchtime, I went back upstairs, thoughtfully, to see if I could sense the ghost hound again. She was in the bedroom, still under the bed, and I felt her nose in my hand again as she crept out. It's not easy to stroke a ghost; you tend to stroke *through* rather than around but we managed something and she seemed to enjoy it.

'You should have a name,' I said to her. 'I can't just call you "ghost hound."'

I knew I should call Robbie, my fellow exorcist, and Alessina, my best friend and our local witch, to tell them about the twins but it was my day off so I shelved it, just for the moment and, instead, looked up the address of the West Devon Hunt and pootled on down to see what I could discover.

The Master of Foxhounds was a woman, Teresa (without an 'h'). I'm weirdly talented at being able to tell how people's names are spelled even when they just speak them out loud. It may have something to do with having been lumbered with the names Phaedra Amabel Velvet at birth. It's possible that, had my parents not died in a car crash, I might just have had to kill them. That's a joke, by the way. Vicars *are* allowed to make jokes, whatever their bishops may think.

It's my experience that country folk are a lot more fey than most of us expect, though they'll hide their knowledge of the land and its spirits under a good old-fashioned hard-boiled covering that takes few prisoners. Looking into Teresa's justly-suspicious blue eyes (she wasn't a church-goer so didn't know me and I could have been a hunt saboteur), I decided to come out with the full weird and asked her if she could remember a creamy-coloured hound who had died after having puppies.

'Yes, *Seraphim,*' she said, immediately. 'Why?'

Of course, she would be named after one of the highest

hierarchy of angels, wouldn't she? I saved that chuckle for later and, in an astonishing moment of high good sense which went so against the grain that I could almost taste a tree trunk in my mouth, I forbore to tell her that *Seraphim* is a plural. The hound should have been called *Seraph*.

'Someone reported seeing a ghost hound,' I said, totally but not completely honestly.

Teresa stared. 'A *ghost* hound?' What?'

'Animals have souls too,' I said, helplessly.

'Well, of course they do!' her tone was impatient. 'But why would they be ghosts?'

'She died after having puppies,' I said. 'Maybe she wasn't willing to leave them.'

'Oh.' Teresa considered. 'That's horrible. I hate that thought.'

'I know,' I said. 'I hate it too. So, I want to do all I can to help her go through.'

'How do you know she died after having puppies?'

That was a very good question. I could have kicked myself.

'It's just a sense I got,' I said, foolishly.

Teresa, a tall, handsome woman in jodhpurs, boots and Barbour, softened. 'I was very fond of Seraphim,' she said. 'She was a lovely hound. Would you like to see a picture of her?'

'Yes please.'

We walked together into Teresa's kitchen and she picked up her tablet, scrolling through a load of pictures of horses and foxhounds. 'Here she is,' she said, showing me not a photograph but a video of a laughing, tail-wagging hound with a cream face and body, golden ears and the most beautiful loving dark brown eyes.

'Tell me more about this ghost,' said Teresa. 'And can you take me to see her?'

Chapter Four

'You don't have to go anywhere,' I said. 'She's here, now.'

It wasn't the brightest thing to say, I know. Small case of foot-in-mouth disease. But I wasn't fibbing. The ghost hound was standing right beside me; I could feel her nose in my hand. I don't know a lot about ghosts—at least, not about earthbound souls; heavenly souls are a different matter—but it seems that dog souls at least can move around, even if only when attached to a human.

Teresa gave me an old-fashioned look. '*Really...?*' she drawled.

'Help!' I sent up to whatever passing angel or deity might be available, and an answer came.

'Do you have any of her puppies still?' I asked. 'I know this is all very weird but, if you've got the time to show me one of Seraph-*im*'s puppies... [it hurt, it *hurt!* But that was her *name*]... perhaps they would react to her?'

'I don't have ti...' said Teresa, who was suddenly interrupted by a rash of barking and howling. At least four hounds had lifted their voices in excitement. Seraph*im* raced towards the source of the sound and so did I, leaving Teresa to follow, expressing exasperation through every pore.

We rounded a corner to the stables that housed both horses and hounds and two men in workman-like riding outfits looked at me curiously.

'Who's yelling?' said Teresa.

'Eden, Eve and Emblem,' replied one of the men. 'How do, Rev. Amabel.'

It was Chris Oakham, a regular church attendee and stalwart of the annual fête. I knew he was a local farmer but had had no idea he was a part of the hunt.

'Hi Chris,' I said. 'And hello to you too, Sir,' to the other man.

'Are Eden, Eve and Emblem daughters of Seraphim?' (it was getting easier…)

'Seraphim?' said Chris. 'Yes. We lost her earlier this year. Why?'

'Look,' I said. The big barn door was open with the straw-filled pens inside visible. Five hounds were circling each other by the door, sniffing and squeaking with pleasure. If you looked at the dance with peripheral vision, you could see that in the middle there was a constant hound-shaped space, dancing with her puppies.

It all went downhill from there, obviously. Teresa and the two men didn't see what I could perceive and it was pretty obvious that there was no point in explaining. But I was a vicar; you have to be polite to vicars though, sadly, you certainly don't expect them to be spiritual or to see ghosts. They acknowledged that the five hounds who were dancing and squeaking were Seraphim's puppies—two from a previous litter and three from the one where she died. But that was a just a coincidence, obviously.

I made my excuses and left, not knowing if the ghost hound would stay or come with me. But, at least, I now had confirmation of who she was. Seraphim turned up in the front seat of the car just as I drove back through the village—she was getting easier to perceive with every minute—and seemed to enjoy watching the unreal world go by. At home, she established herself on the sofa in my living room. Obviously ghosts still appreciate comfort!

Yes, I know it was my day off but I made the mistake of checking emails… so vicarly administration was the order of the rest of the day and I did manage to get a quick phone call in with Robbie, my former assistant vicar, now working in the Fens, and with my current assistant, Lucie. Both of them had experience of the dark side; both had been possessed during the strange events of the previous year when Robbie and I had been part of a group of exorcists set up by my late fiancé, Bishop Paul Joans. That group had dissipated after his death but Robbie was still willing to do the work, in theory at least. Lucie had wanted to put the whole idea of demons behind her and pretend it had never happened, probably because she was never a member of that group; she replaced Robbie when he moved to his own parish and accidentally walked into a rather nasty can of worms. Lucie's character is as lovely as her face and she is one of the world's true innocents as well as being slightly dyslexic. Her texts are a source of both confusion and joy in my life. I turned autocorrect off on my phone in about 2008 and type out words in full but Lucie sends texts that read, 'RU horny? Can bring penis. Lesbian the horse in 10,' which generally means, 'Are you hungry? I can bring pizza. Leaving the house in ten minutes.'

One of my favourites was when she confided that she was 'using masturbation to clear her inner lemons.' I assume she meant "meditation" and "demons" but I didn't have the heart to ask. She would have been mortified.

I told Robbie my concerns about the twins but he was more inclined to blame it on childish wilfulness, before spending a good ten minutes banging on about the undisciplined behaviour of children in church at a recent wedding he had conducted. I had some sympathy with him; it's not easy to hold a space of sanctity with kids running up and down the aisle, screaming, but most folk wanting a church wedding nowadays are after the occasion rather than the spirit. The Church has no one to blame but itself; its teachings are set in stone, party lines are toed (despite regular debates about LGBTQ issues that, except for the Methodists—God bless 'em—have been getting next-to-nowhere) and the world has moved on to the deep and sincere worship of Mammon.

Lucie, who was prepping for a funeral, had observed nothing untoward in the twins and happily discounted my experience, saying I was probably tired. I hoped she was right, and said so, but I knew she wasn't. Lucie was always prepared to see the best in the world and, because of her beauty, most folk were willing to reflect that back to her as well. She was incredibly popular and constantly kind and willing and therefore cruelly over-worked by half the parish. We weren't quite "Reverend Nice and Reverend Nasty" but if you had the choice between a wide-eyed spaniel puppy and a war-weathered Rottweiler, the odds are that you'd call the puppy if you needed a clerical cuddle.

Innocence and kindness won't defend you from the forces of darkness but hey, those are all fictional anyway, say the folk who binge-watch vampire, zombie and apocalyptic TV shows without realising how many secret doors they are opening to the Void.

Lucie popped in later that afternoon (I show up; Lucie '*pops in*') and we had a cup of tea together with scones slathered with butter and topped with Alessina's lovely hedgerow jam, full of vitamin C with blackberries, elderberries, sloes, rowan, hawthorn and rose hips. As Lucie poured herself a second cup of tea from my old, scarred brown china teapot, a bright red berry in the jam on her plate caught my eye. Its colouring and shape were distinctive and, without a word of apology, I scooped it up with my knife. Yes, I was right, it was a yew berry—or aril—but there was no stone in it. Phew! I knew Alessina could be trusted and that the aril itself was harmless but it was still a bit shocking to see. A yew stone is poisonous—pretty much anything from a yew tree is highly toxic apart from the soft red aril itself.

'Sorry,' I said, after the event. 'I was surprised to see that berry in the jam. I didn't think Alessina used yew.'

'*Yew?"* Lucie's reaction was swift but dainty; she deposited her mouthful of scone into a piece of the kitchen towel which doubled as napkins in my kitchen and put it straight in the bin. 'That's poisonous, isn't it? What do we do? What do we *do?*' Her hands began to shake and her soft brown eyes filled with tears and I wondered, not for the first time, whether demonic possession could lead to PTSD. There isn't a lot of information on the subject. Lucie was both one hundred per cent adorable and prone to over-reacting. Mind you, over-reacting is probably the best thing to do with the imminent threat of being poisoned.

'It's okay,' I said. 'It's only the seed in the berry that's poisonous. The berry itself is fine. I'm sorry I scared you.'

But neither of us fancied any more jam and I promised my still-twitchy assistant to check out the ingredients with Alessina. Fortunately, there was still plenty of last year's honey from the bees in our churchyard hives so we were still able to enjoy an alternative, slightly sticky afternoon tea with no apparent side-effects from the already-eaten jam. I had a quick Google on my iPad to show Lucie any potential symptoms of yew poisoning so she could feel reassured that she didn't have any.

Even so, I was glad that I was due at Alessina's for supper that evening, despite the sudden rainstorm that made the walk down to her witch's cottage more of a torch-lit squelch than a stroll. We live on the edge of Dartmoor—literally on the border of open moorland—and the peaty soil makes waterproof walking shoes or wellies a necessity for most people for a good half of the year. I was suitably covered by a showerproof coat from the local charity shop and arrived only slightly damp. The wet brought gloom to the grey, willow-overhung footpath by the stream that giggles its way past Alessina's crooked stone cottage. Just as I arrived the rain stopped, leaving natural water-droplet Christmas lights glistening in the hedges and the apple trees throughout the garden, illuminated by the cosy orange light beaming through her ground-floor windows.

This is a witch's cottage, crouching into a hillside with old speckled-glass windows and troughs of herbs by the unlocked front door. Water loves to drip down your neck from the thatch as you stand in the porch, ringing the cowbells on the lintel to announce your arrival. Once inside, the narrow hallway leads to a kitchen swathed in hanging dried herbs, filled with woven baskets, draped with hops, stuffed with jars of dried teas and fermented vegetables and decorated with feathers, birds' nests and bones on the windowsill. A kettle was singing on a tiny old range and a note lay on the old, scarred table in the middle of the room. Alessina was down at the chicken coop and would be back in a few minutes.

I wandered around the room, enjoying the ambience and wondering what it must be like to live in such harmony with nature that the very plants themselves call 'pick *me*' when you walk past. Most plants, if they could, would emulate the small prey animals of this world and run away when a human comes along but Alessina is the epitome of the *honourable harvest.* She never picks the first, nor the last, she gives back in the form of libations of home-made dandelion wine or a pinch of oatmeal or corn, dropped onto the earth, and she only picks the plants that give her permission to do so.

How does she know? People like Alessina are tuned to a different wavelength from the rest of us. She does talk to the trees—and listens—and first thing every morning, rain, sleet or shine, she goes out to sing a hymn of gratitude to Mother Nature. It's not so very different from Lauds in a monastery or convent; and it's a lovely idea to sing to greet the day. I can't sing but occasionally I drone out the odd verse of *Morning Has Broken* if it is a very sunny day; but I do go into my beautiful old church building every morning to give thanks and bless the peoples of the parishes and Alessina says that's nearly as good—as long as I remember that "peoples" includes the creatures, the vegetation, the weather and the very ground itself.

Talmud, the Jewish commentary on the first five books of the Hebrew Testament, states that every living thing has its own guardian angel, urging it to grow, and these devas or dryads (or whatever you want to call them) are a kind of earth angel and just as worthy of honour as the angels in St. Raphael's, the very archangels of heaven and those in many other sacred spaces and in places such as medical centres, too. If you ever visit someone in hospital, stop by the chapel (though it will probably be called a Peace Room nowadays) and say a prayer of blessing for the angel of that place. Hospital angels are frequently exhausted and an honest prayer of blessing will fluff them up no end. If the angel is strong, the workforce and the patients will respond in kind.

I presume the same goes for government buildings, offices and even homes but I tend to keep that to myself; I wouldn't want people thinking I was weird, now would I?

Alessina's husband, Luke, arrived home first; he is a tall and skinny man with a stack of greying hair and the kind of gnarly hands that can do *anything* creative. Luke makes gallons of dandelion and elderberry wines each year, crafts and paints drums, together with his wife, and works professionally with wood. He made me nearly choke one suppertime when he said that the only thing he really knew for certain about Jesus was that both he and his dad were rubbish carpenters.

'How so?' I asked, in a slightly prickly manner.

'Simple,' said Luke. 'Jesus never mentions carpentry in any of his parables. According to him, the kingdom of heaven isn't like anything in carpentry and no one even mentions furniture apart from a manger—and I doubt Joseph knocked that up while Mary was in labour. If Jesus or his Dad knew what they were doing as carpenters there are loads of wonderful analogies he could have used.'

That was probably the longest string of sentences I ever heard from Luke but, to be fair, I can't remember a lot he has said anyway and I couldn't tell you if that's my memory or his natural quietness. This story, however, stuck because we had some fun with it, discussing whether or not the 'plank in your own eye' in Matthew chapter seven was additional evidence of rubbish carpentry.

'Evening,' Luke said, strolling through the kitchen with his collie, Jamie, on the way to his workroom. The little dog usually attached to his side like a burr but, tonight, Jamie came up to me and sniffed the air around my legs. I'd forgotten about Seraphim but obviously she had come with me and, now, I could feel her tail wagging against my leg.

'Who's this?' said Alessina, coming into the kitchen and looking down at the ghost hound before we could even greet each other.

'You can see her?' I asked. 'She seems to have moved in with me.'

'Yes, she has,' said Alessina. 'That's strange; you're not a particularly doggy person.'

'Apparently she is protecting me,' I said.

'Says who?'

'Erm. Marcus. The Dog Wrangler. From the other side.'

'Oh! *Do* tell me about Marcus,' she asked. 'We've got half an hour before the rest of the family get home and we have to cut back on the crazy.'

So, we settled down at the old wooden table with two mugs of tea and I told her all about Seraphim and Marcus.

If your archetypical description of a witch is a lone woman in a cottage, casting spells and spinning, Alessina breaks that mould. She has two children, a boy and a girl, both full-grown and at college so only home in the holiday times. She did the school run for fourteen years during which no one even outed her as a witch even though she was supplying herbs and tinctures and taking folk on meditative journeys into the underworld while her kids were learning maths and French. But apart from that, my black-haired, natural fibre-clothed friend is all witch. I should emphasise that this is her own self-description. I would call her a wise woman, a forager, a shaman, a nature-lover but then, being a vicar, I couldn't possibly be friends with an *actual* witch, could I?

Alessina can talk to animals, even though she doesn't call herself a dog, horse or bee-whisperer. She can talk to ghost hounds, too, but Seraphim wasn't saying much; she just intimated that she was sticking with me and that she was quite happy about it. She did exude some joy at having seen her children, Alessina said, which was impressive because I hadn't mentioned the trip to the hunt kennels.

'Here's a silly one,' I said. 'Is it okay if I call her Seraph? Her living name was Seraphim and you know what a nerd I am about spelling and grammar and the like.'

'You can call her Spot if you want to,' said Alessina. 'She is aware of your every feeling. She seems to love you.'

'I have no idea why.'

Alessina smiled. 'I'm not sure she has, either,' she said.

Supper was five of us—seven if you count living and ghost dogs. Luke and Raymond, his son, spoke briefly about badgers and cattle and Alessina and Ruth, her daughter, discussed how Christmas went and the phenomenon of transgender chickens—which is a definite thing and, trust me, they're not just doing it to be fashionable. I didn't mention Seraph again because even wonderful husbands and children of witches have their limits and, after we had eaten a herby tray bake of root vegetables with soft cheese from Luke and Alessina's own goats and vegetable patch, Alessina and I went into her healing room, leaving Luke and Raymond to catch up on the football and Ruth to hang out on WhatsApp.

'I have to talk to you about jam,' I said. 'Do you put yew arils in your hedgerow jam?'

Alessina looked over the top of her reading spectacles. She

was winding some wool onto her spinning wheel; she liked to spin as we talked. The whirr-whirr-clack was as soothing as a lullaby.

'No,' she said. 'I wouldn't risk it. I know the berries are safe but even one scratching of a pit could give someone a bit of an upset and most people think the whole berry is poisonous. I'd hate to have people running for the hills when opening a jar. Why?'

'Because there was one in the pot I began today,' I said. 'It nearly gave Lucie a heart attack as it was on her scone and I had to grab it just in case there was a pit.'

'That's impossible,' said Alessina. 'Which doesn't mean that it didn't happen.'

(This is why I love that woman. Just read those sentences again).

'Quite,' I replied. 'I brought the jar with me. Shall we have a dig through it?'

'Before we do that,' said Alessina. 'How did you *know* it was a yew aril? The rest of the berries are cooked to the extent it would be hard to tell them apart.'

'Good point. Maybe it wasn't cooked, just stuck in later? Can't say that fills me with reassurance but someone could have done it for a mean joke to frighten me?'

'You didn't notice if the seal was broken?'

'No, Lucie opened it and we were talking.'

'Hmmm.' Alessina closed her eyes and spun her wool. I sat silently, happy to wait.

After a few minutes, she sighed.

'There's a hornet in the hive,' she said. 'I can feel it. I wondered what the impression I was getting was these last few days. Someone has opened a door somewhere.'

Together, we went back out to the kitchen, emptied the jar onto a plate and poked through the ingredients. There was one more yew aril, without its pit, about a quarter of the way down.

'I'll have to do a product recall,' said Alessina. A sad joke as she doesn't give many jars away. 'But I'm not telling fibs; this *is* pretty impossible. Look—a totally uncooked aril in the middle of fully-cooked jam. That takes some doing.'

'I wondered if it was Mrs Tiggy's grandchildren,' I confessed.

'They don't like me and they are little horrors. I saw something nasty looking out of their eyes this morning.'

'Possessed children? Hmmm. I doubt it,' said Alessina. 'But we can't rule anything out, can we?'

No, we couldn't rule anything out…

Alessina and I looked long and hard at each other.

'It's starting again, isn't it?' I said.

'Yes,' said my friend. 'It almost certainly is.'

Chapter Five

THE NEXT DAY was the "dress properly, file your nails, do something sensible with your hair" sort. That's because it was also "meet the new bishop" day.

We'd had a temporary bishop for the previous few months while the permanent incumbent was being selected. As I'd been a bit of a celebrity during that time—a vicar being tried for attempted murder does tend to get into the news especially when it is a case that turns itself inside out, exposing a paedophile ring and exonerating said vicar quite dramatically—and the temporary bishop had been somewhat in awe of the situation which meant he had been polite and spent as much time as possible avoiding me like the plague.

It was the now promoted Detective Inspector Eleanor Marks who had mapped out the trap for the paedophiles but I had been instrumental in accidentally recording the whole, dramatic shebang in the cathedral where the men were trying to make it look as though I had taken my own life. They had succeeded with a similar plan with the bishop before me and they would have achieved it again had it not been for Will.

Will is a further complication in my life. He was a homeless man, a former soldier with PTSD from Iraq who, like many, felt abandoned by the system after his discharge and whose life had come apart as he fell through horribly predictable holes in the state support system. He was dozing on the steps of the Edinburgh Woollen Mill in the Cathedral Close when I set off on my ridiculous crusade to try and catch a demon in the great church itself. I beat the demon because it was rubbish at spelling and it tried to curse Faydra Annabel instead of Phaedra Amabel but I couldn't protect myself from its human minions.

Instead, Will saved my life after noticing that the cathedral lights were on at night and wanting to see what was going on. He was probably only interested in whether he could curl up, inside, in a warmish corner for a reasonable night's sleep but instead he found a terrified woman in a white alb, crouched in the nave of the cathedral, beaten and bruised and with a broken arm. Beside her was one man whom she had knocked unconscious with a handy crucifix and, in the vestry, were two other men, sorting out a handy noose with which to string her up.

There wasn't any dramatic shoot-out at the end; Will simply locked the vestry door with the men inside and helped me out of the cathedral. It was the only time that I can remember in my life when I fainted, not that that means anything; with such a patchy memory, I wouldn't know if I had been swooning right left and centre for years. Mind you, I've not swooned since.

The man I had clocked with the crucifix—Detective Chief Inspector Johnson—was silly enough to press charges of assault against a short, tubby female vicar with a broken arm. It's quite useful to know that demons can be stupid and the people they infest can also be so dim that they take on the banality of the demon. And yes, demons are banal; they are clichéd, commonplace, cruel and they need to feed on human energy in order to survive. They aren't choosy but they do love a deep vein of resentment and blame in which to lay their eggs.

My fortunate mistake of turning on the recording equipment in the cathedral together with the lights, and Eleanor Marks's integrity in believing in me, meant she found the recording and kept it safe. A clever barrister used a legal loophole to keep it secret until the start of the trial; it brought the dramatic turn-around we needed and, since then, six men have been jailed for both murder and paedophilia.

Which left me with the offer of a spectacular tell-all book deal and a formerly-homeless guy who had saved my life and who deserved a little TLC himself.

It took me all of a day to turn down the book idea; I'm far too much of a snob to go the tabloid newspaper way and far too much of a control freak to have someone help ghost-write my story. I'll write about faith, magic or miracles but I'm not going to play the celebrity game. Yes, the money might have been fabulous but not the price. I'm totally blessed in that I have my little, happy home and I don't need to have much truck with the temptations of Mammon. A wise person once said about the uber-wealthy that the one thing they can never seem to have is 'enough' so those who *do* have enough are far happier than they.

Will, however, gave the press all the time that they could pay for. I can't blame him (though I did!); he desperately needed a fresh chance in life and money is certainly a help with that. It wasn't so bad until the papers started speculating that we might be in a relationship and Will decided that would be an excellent idea, too.

He was nice, he was kind, he was attractive, he was ten years younger than me which is flattering but... And there were a lot of buts. The main one was that even though I can't remember much about being engaged to the previous dearly-departed bishop, I wasn't ready for a new start.

No, I didn't lead him on but yes, you could think that in finding him a place to stay and encouraging him to lean on the church for help could be interpreted that way...

I only have patchy recall of Paul's and my relationship. There are times when I do feel a deep grief for his death, which is nearly a year ago now, but it's a visceral, unconscious thing and strangely unreal. A grief that bites when you can't actually remember why is as disconcerting as it is painful. I can't even recall if Paul chose my engagement ring or if we did it together.

So, I wasn't ready... and I certainly wasn't ready for a relationship with someone who was potentially even crazier than me.

I got some counselling after the trial. It was probably pretty pointless because there was no way that I was going to tell any therapist about angels, demons or exorcisms. But what little I did tell her freaked her out anyway and she thought I was doing a lot of hallucinating caused by a head injury. Maybe I was; maybe I still am; maybe the whole travelling through the stars thing with my dead brother is just a fantasy but, if it is, it's a damn fine one and it's not doing anybody any harm.

Alessina sent me to her friend Philip who worked with kinesiology and something called Emotional Freedom Therapy and, once I'd tried both, I was astonished at how many tears I shed about my parents all those years later and all my unacknowledged anger about Paul's death.

I sent Will to Philip. He didn't like it.

'You're a *vicar!* You shouldn't go for this New Age crap!' he said. It's odd how the sentence, 'you're a *vicar!*' is always followed by 'you shouldn't…' as if vicars were less than human. Okay, I know we're supposed to err on the side of the angels but we still have to live on a very uptight planet.

He's right, at least he's right in his opinion that most people think that a vicar shouldn't go for anything other than pure Christianity. But there's not a lot of pure Christianity around. What there is, is Christianity-Within-The-System—and the system is exclusive. I consistently tell people that Jesus was a healer and that he told us to continue to be healers. He never told us *how* to be healers and the modern world seems to think that allopathic medicine is the be-all and end-all. If I were a "proper" vicar, I should be able to heal the way Jesus did. I can't and I'm very glad that there are people who can. I don't need them to be Christians for one simple reason: Jesus wasn't a Christian. He was a Jew.

Of course, you get Jewish folk objecting to complementary therapies, too, and I'm sure there are many folk practising alternative medicine who are not crammed to the gunnels with integrity and there are horror stories for sure… but I've met some pretty bad doctors, too. All I can say for certain is that Philip's healing techniques helped me considerably. And, although Will got the best medical treatment available, including psychiatry, and he did manage to find a proper home to call his own and began to train in IT, he wasn't the man he wanted to be or believed that he used to be.

There's a strange truism that the rescuer loves the rescued but the rescued wants to move on. The rescuer gets self-esteem from their action and often wants to go on rescuing. Will now wanted to rescue me from the horrors of alternative medicine and, as for my friendship with Alessina, 'Bella, she's *a witch!*'

Yes, she is; a damn fine one too. And a better Christian-in-action than I'll ever be.

Will comes to supper about once a fortnight; there's no possibility that is going to stop any time soon; he wants to come and, despite his new Evangelical tendencies (he's even thinking of doing the Alpha course, God help him), he's good company with a wicked sense of humour. He's easy on the eye, too, with soft brown, wavy hair, dark grey eyes and, now he's back getting fit again, a fluidity of movement that is both slightly intimidating and attractive.

If I were a Jewish mother, I'd have plans for him and Lucie and, it's fair to say, the three of us have some lovely, easy-going suppers together where I do feel somewhat like Mum, but in a good way. Probably in a control-freak kind of way, really, as I am the Rector after all.

But time has moved on; Bishop Paul's full-time replacement is here and wanting to meet his team Rectors individually at the Bishop's Palace in Exeter. I suppose he wanted to get to know each one of us before he had to rally the troops—and even more likely, before the new Dean arrived, too. We're still waiting on that news. The old Dean, by the way, simply retired; he wasn't infested or weird or magical or unusual, just long-suffering and increasingly knackered.

A meeting with the new Bishop seemed sensible, not least because Devon is one of the small corners of the world where black folk and those, like me, who are currently known as "people of colour" (but that terminology might change any minute), aren't exactly the majority. Prejudice is often unconscious and subtle and, stupidly, also thrives between different shades of black and brown.

Devon's First Black Bishop the headlines trumpeted. Maybe one day there won't be a need to point that sort of thing out but it's not coming any time soon. A lot of folk have been saying "all the right things" about the new bishop but very few realise that the Church of England, like so many white patriarchal organisations, still play the "welcome to the party" game from the point of view that it's still *their* party and how great it is that others have now been invited. Jesus wasn't like that; he made it clear that *everyone* was invited to God's party no matter what colour, race, gender, sexuality, ability or profession. I like Jesus. A lot. But even though I'm a part of it, I'm not always that fond of his fan club.

Bishops are generally a little scary, well-meaning and fairly politically streetwise. They have to be practical as well as faithful. Sometimes, they click with all their clergy; sometimes they have to try hard not to be cliquey with the ones they do get on with or with whom they share the same level of faith… and sometimes they simply don't fit and make life a misery for everyone.

I was feeling pretty nervous before the meeting but, to be fair, I expect he was a tad on the apprehensive side too. When one of your vicars has been involved in a high-profile court case, was the cause of several other members of the area's clergy being jailed and happened to be engaged to your predecessor, it's going to take quite some bishop not to be slightly concerned about her ability to take orders and fall into line. And when half her parishioners love her and the other half think she should be burned at the stake, not to mention when she's written more books than you, the story gets even more challenging.

'So…' said the Right Reverend Xavier Morel as we shook hands in the Bishop's Palace. 'You appear to think you are a Catholic.'

Good start. Not.

Few bishops like a smart-arse so, with immense self-control, I forbore to mention that his very name was Catholic. The first known Xavier was Saint Francis Xavier, co-founder of the Jesuit order, who got his name from the Spanish-Basque village where he was born.

'Um,' I said, intelligently, instead.

'Exorcisms, Latin, angels…' He waved his arms about expressing astonishment, exasperation and disbelief far more succinctly than finishing the sentence could have done.

'I am certainly "Catholic" in its original sense of "universal,"' said this smart-arse, provoked beyond tact. 'I am perhaps a tad more High Church than is normal here and yet, in other ways, more liberal so it kind of pans out.'

Bishop and Rector locked eyes and both registered simultaneous shock, attraction and utter dislike. How do I know that? Because I *am* far more Catholic than I "should" be and sometimes you can just tell.

At least this one was alive. Being still slightly in love with one dead man and vaguely falling in love with a ghost meant life was already over-complicated…

No belief, said Hero in my ear. Well, she didn't say it in my ear; she said it in my mind. Hero, remember, is my guardian, the one Marcus could see (oh Lord, I'm starting to bring Marcus into everything, aren't I?). Yes, I talk to angels. I've been able to do that for more than a year now, ever since what's known as my "near-death experience" which basically means that you died but the other side didn't want you.

'Er … it was an angel who told Mary she was to be the mother of Jesus,' I said out loud. 'My church is named after St. Raphael, the healing angel, and our cathedral has a chapel dedicated to St. Gabriel.' I was aware by now that Hero and Xavier's guardian angel were communicating around and through us. Angels don't *chat* but they do share what we would call "feelings." Except we wouldn't because, to us, feelings are warm blood-filled things and angel communication is bloodless, like cold silver flowing. That's the best way I can put it.

Holding, said Hero and I knew she meant that the two guardians were channelling peace between Xavier and me. He might not believe in angels but he was susceptible to his own.

'Indeed,' said the bishop. 'But I am an Evangelical and not a fan of the Roman Church.'

I bit my lip. *Evangelical* could mean a range of things from Will-like condemnation of alternative medicine, through closed-in, tribal thinking to happy-clappy. It often meant law over *lore* which meant that my friendship with the local witch was probably not going to go down well here either. But to be fair, most bishops aren't fans of witches and, given the general standard of the would-be witches I have met, in purple dresses with too many buttons, pentangle pendants and silver-skull rings, I am somewhat in agreement about that.

Alessina, as I hope I have already shown, is an exception; a genuine wise woman and a fellow exorcist but I could see that we wouldn't be talking about any of that in the Bishop's Palace for the foreseeable future…

'Do sit down,' said his Grace. 'Would you care for some tea?'

As it was eleven AM I was, reluctantly, impressed. People usually offer coffee in the mornings nowadays but I am an inveterate tea-drinker.

'Yes please. Builder's tea, a little milk, no sugar,' I said, still standing and, foolishly equating him with my previous bishop who would encourage you to follow him to his private kitchen and put on the kettle himself.

The bishop rang the bell and one of his assistants put her head round the door. He ordered tea and biscuits and we sat on the edge of our armchairs making polite, if slightly awkward, conversation about the weather and whether people were making him feel welcome, until it arrived. She brought tea in a pot, a hot water jug, a separate milk jug and scones with butter and jam, all in beautiful, matching bone china that was definitely vintage.

'Builder's tea, milk, no sugar,' the bishop said, pouring the milk into my cup first.

Four things happened simultaneously and it will take longer to explain them than they took to occur.

Firstly, I leant forward and said, 'no!' slightly more assertively than intended, in order to stop my tea being pre-drowned in lactose.

Secondly, I noticed the ramekin filled with fruit jam containing a yew aril and my whole body tensed with an adrenaline shock.

Thirdly, I saw a flash of red and felt a warning shout in my head.

Fourthly, with a sound as shocking as a bomb, a brick shattered the window to my left and struck the bishop on the side of the head. He dropped like a stone onto the crimson carpet.

But the fourth thing didn't happen. I experienced it happening but it was a vision, not a reality.

Time had slipped; it was *about* to happen and my body was already moving.

I hurled myself across the table, knocking everything to the ground and pulling the bishop off his chair so that we fell to the floor together in a crumpled heap.

The crash happened simultaneously and the part of me that was more awake than the everyday me ever could be observed the trajectory of the brick as it passed about two feet above the top of the chair that the bishop had been sitting in. It would have struck him on the forehead. A second brick smashed through the window, aimed at where I had been sitting, and hit the carpet inches away from my left arm, showering us with glass.

The first brick, I could see, had a message taped to it. 'Go back where you come from, ******' it said.

'That'd be Croydon,' my shocked brain thought, though I knew perfectly well what it meant. What concerned me more, even than the blatant racism and destruction, was the nature of the attack. No random vandal could aim two bricks through a window with such accuracy.

Shit. It looks like the demons *are* back.

His Grace groaned. He had a gash on his forehead from flying glass. Scrambling to my feet, I staggered over to the door registering, to my surprise, that it was quite hard to move. And then noting with even more discomfort that, instead of being able to grasp the handle, my arm went straight through the panelling.

That sort of thing would give anyone pause for thought. For a moment, I stood there with a fried brain and then, just as someone did knock on the door and then opened it *through me*, I turned around to see my physical body, which was still lying on the floor in an undignified embrace with a groaning bishop.

Chapter Six

I WASN'T DEAD. I was barely hurt. I was told to take a holiday and referred to a counsellor. Why? Because there were no bricks; there was no broken window and no blood. All that had happened was that the mad, hallucinating Rector had made a lunge for the incumbent bishop and knocked him over backwards.

We were both stunned and I simply didn't know what reality I was in for quite a few minutes. Xavier got up before I did as I took a full minute getting back into my body. It wasn't entirely keen to have me back as it thought, quite justifiably, that when I was in there, it either got seriously embarrassed or hurt.

People flooded into the room and one of me watched as they exclaimed in horror at the broken window, the blood and the glass everywhere. Another of me watched as they exclaimed in horror at the mess of spilled tea, shattered crockery and scarlet jam on the bishop's face and in the carpet while the window remained resolutely unbroken and the floor shockingly lacking in bricks. A third me saw a shadow that laughed.

Self-defence mechanisms locked in pretty swiftly once I'd come to myself, been picked up and dusted down. I remembered the yew aril, using it as an excuse for my actions: I was afraid the bishop would be poisoned, I said, so I lunged to stop him eating the scone. Of course, no one found a yew aril and I doubt anyone looked very carefully because why would there be such a thing in a pot of strawberry jam made by one of the cathedral canons?

At least, my story excused me from any accusation that I was attacking the bishop wilfully. But it gave wonderful weight to the idea that I was mentally unstable ('how could she not be, poor thing, after that terrible accident followed by that inexplicable event in the cathedral and the pressures of a trial?') There wasn't a lot I could say because spouting off about premonitions, angels, demons and laughing shadows wasn't exactly going to help.

They let me go home although there was a lot of susurration. Foolishly, I tried to re-arrange the meeting with the shocked and slightly-bruised bishop but that was because I hadn't quite realised how seriously everyone was taking the issue of this Rector's mental health.

I was anxiously looking forward to telling Jon about it and getting his views that night.

But Jon didn't come.

The shock was palpable. He had shown up practically every night for nearly a year and we negotiated what nights we took off. The last thing he had said to me on the previous evening was, 'See you tomorrow.'

There was absolutely nothing I could do. When it comes to the celestial worlds there aren't any telephones, no social media and no online news that you could, at least, check for accidents. I knew it was unlikely that something had happened to Jon himself — his already being dead and all that — but you never know. I certainly didn't. If you were 100% mystic or a psychic or something, I guess you could find out but I'm neither.

By the time I was sure he wasn't coming (or for that matter, he had come and I simply couldn't perceive him), it was far too late to call Alessina—the only other person in the world who knew about Jon and me and also the only other person in the world who might be able to help. Instead, I curled up in bed and slept fitfully. Only at about three AM did I realise that there was no ghost hound around either.

I woke at six after an appalling night's sleep and hi-tailed across to the church in the very first light of dawn. St. Raphael's is a lovely little Norman building with a square tower containing a full set of seven bells, stone effigies of local toffs who fell off their perches with enough cash for a tomb in the church and an old wooden icon in the lady chapel that makes Mary look like a woman from the Middle East rather than a white middle-class British aristocrat with a button mouth. St. Raphael's also has the most beautiful dark wooden rood screen protecting the ancient golden triptych behind the altar. I've been campaigning to get that rood screen unlocked outside service time for years but the Parish Council's protective views are winning so far.

St. Raphael's is a short walk across the graveyard next to my house and the hills of Dartmoor rise up behind it. Where I live used to be the village Rectory but now it's the "Old" Rectory and it is my personal property; not that of the Church. The new and official church residence is down the road in the row of houses built about ten years ago and Lucie lives there.

As I unlocked the church door, my heart was in my mouth. You see, ever since the car accident, I've been able to perceive and hear the angel of the church, whose name is Ariel. All churches have their own angel, as do all hospitals, all cities, all countries and all planets but mostly, especially nowadays, they are faded and dusty and no one knows they are there.

I never knew either until the accident but, since then, visiting the church has been magical because every time I say a service, I can perceive the angel song that always accompanies it. That lifts everything and, I swear, I have never spoken a liturgy on automatic since.

Today, I couldn't perceive her and my heart sank.

'Ariel?'

Sometimes she takes a holiday in the Lady Chapel but she's always around somewhere. I looked and called for far longer than was sensible, illogically thinking that had she been there, she would have responded. She *did* hide under the lady chapel altar once but that was only when a demon was visiting.

But, hang on a minute, angels *are.* I've learnt that. They *are* there whether you can perceive them or not.

So, was it me? Had I lost my ability to see and hear other dimensions? How did that happen? And even more importantly, how did I get it back?

Until your life is infused with spiritual magic, it is hard to imagine how empty the world might seem without it. I heard tell that Mother Teresa prayed to know what it might be like to live without faith and subsequently lost it so that she genuinely would know how the majority of people felt. Now, I'm no Mother Teresa but if she felt anything like the sense of loss and despair that I faced that morning, then how she continued with her work I simply don't know.

Normally, I'm a breakfast girl. And an elevenses girl. And possibly a rather suspiciously-early lunch so we can focus on afternoon tea girl. But today, my appetite was gone; I hadn't even had my normal tea and biscuit in bed. Instead, with a hole in my heart the size of Manchester, I set off for the other end of the village and Alessina's cottage.

She was out, of course, so I sat on the stone steps to the cottage and worried.

After five minutes, I pulled myself back together and began to pray. About time really. Prayer is very under-used as a self-help practice and I have no idea what my prayer life was before the accident but since… well, let's just say that if you are experiencing miracles daily you are more inclined to trust in prayer and prayer, in turn, is more likely to find you trustworthy, too.

For me, it's mostly about focusing on clearing my mind and heart and simply listening. Yes, of course there are times that I ask and in church services I have to do a lot of praying out loud but, when I'm alone, more often than not I just try to stay open to whatever is on offer. Some days, if you listen deeply enough, you can hear the music of the spheres. I told Robbie, my former assistant, that once and he replied, 'No, that's tinnitus.'

Sitting on Alessina's doorstep, surrounded by her dormant, edible garden, I focused inwards and asked God, 'What if anything, do I need to know right now?'

Nothing occurred for quite a few minutes and then I heard buzzing. I opened my eyes but there was nothing obviously visible—and as it was still the heart of winter there shouldn't have been any bee or wasp around.

The hornet rose out of a rosemary bush. I could tell that it wasn't physically real; it was blurred… and surely far too big? It hovered menacingly and, looking at it, I felt a far deeper fear than just one insect should have been able to engender.

This was what prayer had brought me? I felt a wave of self-pity and then, strong and clear, the awareness that this was exactly what the hornet wanted.

'*Hero!*' I whispered and, for one precious moment, I knew that my guardian angel was still there.

That was it, though. Just one inkling. However, it was enough. I could still perceive the spirit world, even if only momentarily. It didn't solve the problem of a large, possibly imaginary, hornet, though.

That was sorted by St. Patrick's Lorica—or, at least, the version that I use as it comes in several forms.

'Christ be with me, Christ within me, Christ behind me, Christ before me, Christ beside me, Christ to win me, Christ to comfort and restore me. Christ above me, Christ below me, Christ in quiet, Christ in danger, Christ in the hearts of all who love me, Christ in the mouth of friend and stranger.

'I bind unto myself this day the strong name of the Trinity, by invocation of the same the three in one; the one in three. By whom all nature has creation; Eternal Mother, Spirit, Word, praise to the Lord of our salvation; salvation is through Christ.'

I watched the image as I spoke the sacred words out loud and it simply faded away. That gave me a moment's pause for thought; was it still there but now invisible? Or had it gone? But that way madness lay and I was confused enough as it was.

Instead, I sat and waited. Alessina went out just after dawn, most days, to sing to the morning. I have to admit that her form of prayer is quite a bit more beautiful than mine. She sings joy and thanks to all creation in a paeon of praise. I think it's entirely possible if a lot more of us did such things we might all be less depressed and the world might be feeling quite a lot healthier.

And that's when the man came by. He was a woodsman; a stranger to me, possibly a traveller, wearing trousers that once were black and, with age and weathering, were now a perfect camouflage for the woods. His jacket, too, was worn and faded and his beard and hair were long and unkempt but his eyes were bright and kind; possibly Irish ancestry with that vibrant blue?

'You'll be waiting for t'witch, then,' he said, with a twinkle. 'Is it some of her magic you're needing?' The voice was Devonian but I thought it also had a slight Irish cadence.

'Just company,' I said, cautiously. You never know what people think about those they call witches and their associates.

'You'm a Lady of the Yew,' said the man, unexpectedly. 'You've walked the seven circuits.'

He quoted:

> Walk ye backward round about me
> Seven times round for all to see;
> Stumble not and then for certain
> One true wish will come to thee.

The old Devonian rhyme, I knew, came from a legend surrounding the giant yew in the church of St. Mary and St. Gabriel in the Devon village of Stoke Gabriel—about an hour away. But I had no memory of doing such a walk. Not that that meant anything, of course.

'What makes you say that?' I said.

'Ah well, I just knows,' said the man. 'You asked to understand God and I s'pose you got more than you bargained for!' He shook his head, laughing a little. 'Mebbe you needs to do that circuit again. Here—a little sign for you,' he held out a gnarly hand with four yew arils in it. 'I found 'em. Four souls. Knew they was for someone.'

'Oh.' I let him pour the arils into my hand. 'Thank you.'

'They'm lost souls,' said the woodsman. 'Too many legends to tell around the yew, but if these show up, unexpected, they'm a warning. See? They'm trying to tell you something; show you summat.'

'Oh,' I said again.

Blue eyes twinkled at me again.

'You'm thinking I'm crazy,' he said.

'No… no, I don't. But I am confused. I don't know if I have walked the seven circuits or made any such wish.'

'Oh, you have,' he said. 'And the wish wore off. You'm lost without it. Mebbe you should walk it and ask again.'

'Yes. Yes, maybe.' I'd started feeling very uncomfortable with all this talk of warnings and wishes.

'What's your name?' I asked, knowing that I would want Alessina to tell me more about this man.

'Simon,' he answered. 'And that's a heavy cross you're carrying, sweeting. Remember the yew. There'll be summat waiting for you there, for sure.'

He straightened up with a sharp exhalation of breath as if he had a bad back and walked away across Alessina's garden and into the woodland. His clothing guaranteed invisibility in seconds, merging him into the dappled light.

I opened the hand which I had clenched around the arils and looked at them, curiously. Alessina might well be longer and I could easily go back to the churchyard and walk seven times, backwards around the yew tree there. Maybe I'd done that before the car crash? Maybe I had wished understand God. Was that why I started seeing angels? Maybe…?'

My thoughts were broken by the sound of song behind me. Alessina was returning. 'Just in time,' a thought whispered though I must admit I found myself slightly disappointed. I wanted to follow the magic.

Alessina was sparkling light, even in her old raincoat and even older boots. She finished the rippling song of creation before she came in through the little crooked wicket gate at the front of her stone cottage and her smile when she saw me was stronger than sunshine.

'Oh Bel! How lovely. But what is it, darling? What has happened?'

Simon and the arils flew out of my mind; I think I dropped them as I jumped up and went forward for a hug.

'I've lost my vision,' I choked. 'Jon didn't come and I can't see the angels. I don't know what to do.

'How are you…?' I added weakly, having dived in—as I so often do—without considering anyone else but me. Not a characteristic that's normally expected from a vicar, really.

'Tea,' said Alessina, sensibly. 'Linden and hawthorn tea, I think. '

I concurred; I'm a PG Tips girl myself and Alessina's brews can taste quite disgusting but they are healing and powerful and I certainly needed some help.

We didn't discuss anything of consequence while she put the kettle on and brought out a tin of home-made biscuits. I was just so glad that she had time; Alessina works hard at her craft, teaching people to make drums and rattles and taking them on deep, inner journeys to retrieve aspects of their soul, hidden away at times of trauma. It's not exactly like Voldemort and the horcruxes but I expect J. K. Rowling knew something about alchemy.

At last, with hot (not too bad-tasting) tea inside me, I was able to explain what was—or wasn't—going on. My friend listened attentively.

'I don't even know if Seraphim is still with me,' I ended and you can tell how upset I was, just by that.

'I can't sense her,' said Alessina and held my hand. 'She may be back at the house.'

Finally, I told her about Simon and she nodded. 'Simon is a woodsman,' she said. 'I know him quite well. There's no harm to him. Do you still have the arils? This is becoming a bit of a theme, isn't it?'

We went back outside to look for the little red cups but they didn't seem to be there.

'Probably a thrush picked them up,' said Alessina. 'Birds don't digest the seeds.'

We sat almost silently with a second cup of tea. I sighed; it was good to be quiet and to allow the tension to dissolve. "The faith and the love and the hope are all in the waiting," as T. S. Eliot wrote. Now, how did that poem continue…?

'So,' said Alessina. 'Shall we see if we can find this all-important part of your soul and why you sent it away?'

Chapter Seven

I HAD FORGOTTEN to tell Alessina about the hornet.

'There's a hornet in the hive,' she had said. 'Someone has opened a door somewhere.'

I'd seen it. I'd actually *seen* the damn thing. How stupid can you be?

Very stupid, obviously.

I also hadn't insisted that I was right about what I had seen in the twins' eyes. Why on earth not?

We didn't do a soul retrieval session there and then because Alessina has a life and plenty of clients. Who knows how things might have worked out if we had? Instead we set a time for two days later and I went home, feeling a little bit better but still confused.

Mrs. Tiggy met me with a message from the Bishop's palace. Heart sinking, I rang back to discover that I was to receive a formal letter—an injunction even—to get myself some psychiatric treatment for PTSD and to take time off until I was "feeling better." I wasn't suspended; I would still be paid, in the interim at least, but Lucie was to take over my duties for the moment and, if things did not work out as everyone so earnestly hoped, a replacement Rector would be sought.

Crunch time, then.

I sighed. Sighing is such a safety valve, isn't it? I knew that shock and anger would hit me later on but, for the moment, I was still vicar of this parish and I had work to do until the letter actually arrived. It would be a "proper letter", not an email, so there was still time.

This day was set aside for parish visits so I ate some late breakfast, put on the trusty dog collar, a vaguely presentable skirt, shoes that almost matched the outfit *and* each other and set off on my rounds.

Vicaring isn't really about services, communion, weddings, baptisms and funerals, it's about pastoral care. That mostly means listening while drinking a lot of tea and trying not to eat all the biscuits. It's the listening that's the key, not the talking. And then more listening. And, to follow up, a tad more listening. Just occasionally, someone actually does want advice but mostly you just nod and put on your 'oh dear…' face. I was quite good at it, despite my general impatience, mostly because Hero, my guardian angel, would whisper untold truths into my mind while the parishioner was talking. It gave the effect of telling me exactly when, where and why the person was lying or embellishing the truth and because I knew the *why* I could better understand the overall *what*.

It didn't mean I could necessarily help, of course because, let's face it, what would you do if all your problems were taken away? You'd have to be happy and then everyone would hate you.

It seems we feel that we're allowed to be happy on our wedding day, at special events and on holidays but even then, there's that tendency of "just one thing" as in, 'it was lovely but…' almost as though we have to justify our contentment with a problem. And that can open the door to a litany of major or minor complaints. Henry David Thoreau had a point when he wrote that most of humanity lives a life of quiet desperation. I wish it weren't so—and yes, sometimes I have felt guilty about the magic and mystery that has infused my own life when so many have never seemed to experience much joy. But then, hey, they haven't been attacked by demons or had disturbed detective chief inspectors attempting to kill them, so it's swings and roundabouts really…

Obviously, I pray with people—when they let me. I pray for guidance, strength and comfort and today I was praying for myself as much as for the parishioners.

This day, over five visits, to my relief I received insights as usual and I bit my tongue, swallowed my words, reproached myself for my lack of compassion, felt my heart break a little bit and got bitten by a ferret (as usual) at Johnny Percival's. Johnny always had the TCP handy for when Cosmo got out of hand—or more accurately got *into* hand—and reminded me to make sure I got a regular tetanus booster shot. Johnny is ninety-six and Cosmo is all he has left so I always say I don't mind, though my fingers have some interesting scar tissue nowadays.

My last-but-one visit was to another regular, Sandra Collingwood, where I spent an hour resisting the conviction that Sandra's daughter was a paeon of tactfulness in not telling her mother some home truths about her mind-blowing control-freakdom. Sandra seemed to think that 45-year-old Julie should still come for Sunday lunch every single week, should dump "that man" who was "taking up too much of her time" (i.e. taking it away from her mother) and shouldn't be getting involved with anyone anyway, given that she was both "a proper spinster" and, contrarily, "mutton dressed as lamb." Cosmo's teeth began to appear benign in comparison.

Finally, it was a "cheer up, I'm sure it's going to be fine" visit to Judith Monroe, who was just about to have her final fertile eggs implanted by IVF. Judith's husband, Steve, was diagnosed with testicular cancer two years after their marriage and chemo had made him infertile. Sensibly, they had stored his sperm and Judith wanted every prayer and positive thought possible as she went into the last round of hope.

'I know we could adopt,' she said. 'Well, I would…'

I know Steve was opposed to the idea. Bitter family experience of a mis-matched adoption, incomprehension and finally a drug-addled death in his aunt's family had put him off for a lifetime. It was understandable but Judith was a born mother; the kind who would stop and pointed out a goldcrest in the bushes and would read her child to sleep every night.

I'm not good at the "it's going to be fine" work because even though I know the ways of Grace are weird and wonderful, three previous failed attempts carried a heavy weight and I *didn't* know if it would be all right. But I said as much of the right thing as I could and I prayed with Judith while drinking yet another cup of over-milked alleged tea. One day, a vicar will crack and throw dreadful tea in a parishioner's lap. A jury would never convict…

On the way home, I called in at the church house where Lucie lives. She was in and all-a-gush with apologies and concern about being asked to take over from me while I "recovered." I wondered how she knew already but if you ever want to maximise gossip, join a church. "Do not bear false witness" is the ninth commandment and gossip is definitely false witness but, hey, that's the *Old* Testament and Jesus never said anything about any of that, right?

She knew; which meant everyone knew because Lucie would have chattered to anyone who would listen about how unworthy she felt to step into my shoes. Damn.

Lucie is the kind of woman you gaze at in wonder and fall in love with, instantly. She glides through life in an unassailable waft of beauty and grace. She never loses her temper, never grumbles or whines and she is kindness personified. She's also a bit of a ninny because she *knows* she's dyslexic and still never checks her texts. She says she needs *auburn cock rocket* (autocorrect) and relies on it wholeheartedly.

I realise that I'm in the minority with that last opinion of ninny-dom and that I'm probably also grumpy, envious and fractious but, when faced with a demon, Lucie will run screaming while I'll remember to exorcise it and probably hit it with a brick just to make sure. Your choice...

To be fair, Lucie has experienced possession first-hand and, as far as I'm aware, I haven't. We got her through it, Alessina and I, but her way of dealing with the trauma is to deny it. For Lucie, very little of the last year actually happened and as she was, technically, out of it for most of the bad bits, I can understand that. And she is very good for me in many ways because she makes me strive to be kinder. However, it would be good to have an assistant with whom you could actually *talk*.

After about ten minutes of heartfelt reassurances that everything would turn out fine and that people would miss me and that she couldn't possibly replace me and that she hoped I would stay in the Old Rectory so she could get my guidance every day to make sure she was doing things right, I realised that I really *didn't* need yet another cup of tea and I probably *could* do with a holiday away. I headed off home.

Marcus was sitting on the doorstep with a little tan-coloured terrier-type on his lap.

And Seraphim was sitting right beside him.

She got up and trotted over to me, as soon as I got out of the car, and she looked a hundred per cent real: a slender foxhound with a speckled champagne-and-cream coat, dark brown eyes and long paws with even longer claws that were, right that moment, resting on my chest. I'm not a big woman and the weight of her practically knocked me over. She was almost shimmering, she was so gloriously real.

'Whoa!' I said, taking her paws in both hands and looking into those bright, beautiful eyes.

'She's yours,' said Marcus.

'Is she *real?* Come to think of it, are you? What is going on?'

Three very big questions which were likely to have answers that made no sense to me whatsoever.

'I cannot get home at this moment,' said Marcus. 'This happens occasionally. Something has blocked the pathway—I believe you might call it a "traffic jam"? And, until it is re-opened, I have to stay here so I thought I would come and see you. I have never voluntarily walked in one of your streets before. I seem to be visible to people; Micki and I walked here and people wove their way about us. They stared at me which is also new to me. I realise that I am dressed in a way you find unusual.'

He was. He looked like someone from a re-enactment troupe.

'Intuition tells me that I may be here a little longer than usual. May I stay with you, if that is the case?'

'Um…' I said, which I thought pretty articulate given the circumstances. 'Yes. Of course. Well, er… come in. And bring your dog. Is he your dog?'

'At this moment, he is. He died. I came to fetch him but the portal closed. I don't know why.'

'So, he's a ghost?'

'A transitioning soul,' Marcus corrected me but I barely listened because I had just recognised the dog. Micki was the 16-year-old, beloved pet of a young couple in the village with whom I was on nodding acquaintance. They had two young children whom Micki adored and looked after—*had* looked after—like a protective nanny since birth.

They would be heartbroken.

I often get annoyed with people who say, so innocently, that "God is Dog spelt backwards," because I want to spit 'Only in English! Other languages are available!' at them. I even used, sometimes, to tell them that "God" spelled backwards in Haiitian Creole is "Eid Nob"... but the point behind their oh-so-inaccurate comment *is* spot on. Mystical understanding of the Divine knows that It is unconditional love—all the "wrath and punishment" scenarios are human-made—and a dog is a great purveyor of absolute unconditional love. I, on the other hand, am not.

As Marcus looked around my kitchen with great interest, touching all the electrical equipment, the saucepans and—possibly most importantly—the biscuits, I made tea. He seemed to think that he might be able to eat and drink, just like Jon can when he's with me. Tea isn't the answer to everything but it helps us along the road that is.

Except when the other person has never had a brew in their lives and practically spits it out across the table with a face that implies that you tried to feed them minced raw sea slug.

So, I tried coffee. He liked coffee. Phew. He was *boulversé* by chocolate biscuits because chocolate was only a drink and only for the aristocracy in his last days. The idea of everyone being able to get cookies coated with the stuff blew his non-existent socks off. It wasn't until the second chocolate digestive that he accepted how delicious they were as it all, to start with, tasted very odd. I confused him further by telling him that chocolate was like that; you think you can leave it but it sneaks up on you while you're looking in the other direction.

I don't know if you have ever had someone from another century come and visit? I don't mean the twentieth century; I mean hundreds of years ago. There is a lot of explaining to do of things that you never thought you would ever have to clarify. And that's on both sides.

Jokes too don't work very well. My favourite "God's what we used to use before we got the Internet", for example, wasn't going to play out well and neither did Marcus's riddle about a steam engine which he thought was the height of ridiculous modernity.

But we talked and talked and talked. Micki and Seraphim (yes, I have finally given in...) curled up together in front of the Aga and snored gently. Marcus and I could touch, too, just like Jon and I, though Marcus felt very tingly and he said my hand felt like silk. Had he ever actually felt silk? I asked, given his ethnicity and his lives as houseboy or slave in the USA, France and London, and given the fact that my hand is not entirely silk-like.

'Oh yes. I would touch the skirts of the ladies when I could. Velvet, silk, cotton, wool. Their clothing fascinated me. Such beauty held together by such pain.'

'Corsets?' My historical knowledge of women's clothing is limited. Marcus knew them as 'stays' and much of our discussion was taken up with explaining our differing language.

He didn't remember a lot about his last life, and even less about the earlier ones, so the conversation was pretty one-sided but it was fascinating nonetheless. People from the past are much simpler than we are; they knew next-to-nothing about the rest of the world or the complications of life outside their town or village. It was much easier for them to be at peace without all the fuss and bother of the news and the Internet. Yes, there was huge inequality but it appeared that folk didn't worry about it half as much as we do. It was what it was, so you had to make it okay or you would be far more miserable than strictly necessary.

The television terrified him; the downstairs shower fascinated him; the flushing lavatory was a miracle and my mobile phone was incomprehensible.

I cooked him supper—a simple meal of pasta and Mediterranean vegetables with goat cheese—all of which were unfamiliar to him. He ate it but said he was having enough trouble coping with taste buds at all, let alone being able to fully appreciate new foods.

We pondered whether, while he was here, he *needed* to eat and drink and what, if anything, had re-formed his corporeal body. As I'd done plenty of research on Mary of Jesus of Ágreda, a Franciscan Abbess investigated by the Inquisition, I wondered whether he was bilocating but he said he had no sense of his other part in heaven, if that was so.

But... and this was a pretty crazy but... he also said that he was under the impression that there were more than a thousand of him; there had to be in order to ensure that every dog came through safely. And there were more of a million other animal wranglers too. No, he rarely met them but he had seen them. The first time he saw himself—at a place where both dogs and cats were dying—he hadn't even thought it strange. He shrugged; the higher worlds had their own rules and, when you were there, they made perfect sense. It was also possible that there *was* only one of him but that he worked outside of time.

'Like Santa,' I said.

'Who?' said Marcus.

Okay...

It appeared that it was just one Marcus not being able to get back, for the moment at least, so it wasn't too much of a problem—apart, that was, from whatever was happening to the pets currently meant to be on his watch.

Did he sleep? I asked; I wasn't quite sure about the role of sleep on heavenly bodies. Apparently, yes, he would sleep with the dogs and, also, yes you can dream when you are asleep in the other world.

Together, we waited up to see if Jon was coming. I thought Marcus would be able to see him if he did, even if I couldn't. But Marcus said he didn't come.

Eventually, I sent him off to the spare room, with Micki, to try and sleep on Planet Earth and I went to bed in my own room. I felt dead on my feet and slept surprisingly deeply given the amount going on. Seraphim slept on my feet.

In the morning they were all gone. The spare bed was unmade so I hadn't made it all up unless, of course, I'd gone completely crazy and ruffled it up myself.

And so, another day in the average life of a rural vicar went ahead. There was a wedding to prepare and a bereaved family to visit both to offer comfort and to decide on how the funeral should go.

Then another day and another and another, which was a Saturday with two weddings, and then Sunday with church services and briefing Lucie on what needed to be done while I was away. No Jon, no angels, no Seraphim, no Marcus.

Monday was the start of my holiday/suspension but there were no psychiatric appointments available for another month so I was pretty much in limbo until I had been assessed. I was quite glad about that because—counter-productive though it might seem—I was going to have to have my story straight for the expert who would be examining me. How could I possibly be honest and not be sectioned?

Stymied, abandoned and confused, I decided to go on holiday.

I booked two weeks in Israel and Jordan which would have been very nice, if I had ever got there.

Chapter Eight

THE DOORBELL RANG at nine PM. We vicars don't have the option of pretending not to hear inconvenient callers just in case it is a frantic parishioner who genuinely needs help, as opposed to someone who simply wants to complain. Even time-out vicars about to go on holiday feel the same obligation so I sighed, put down my book and got up to answer it.

I really, really didn't want to. The evening had already been filled with parish work. Firstly, two members of the parish council phoned, ostensibly to wish me a happy holiday but really to complain about each other. Then Lucie turned up with a file full of last-minute queries. (A file!). I was expecting her to bring supper so I hadn't cooked but I should have used my brain. It turned out that she had "something to consider for when we meet" in her earlier text not, as it actually said, "something to casserole for when we meet." But, hot supper or not, it was fair enough that she wanted to double-check all the events over the next month, "in case you are having so much fun you decide to stay away longer"—how tactful—and discuss a few possible sticking-points with the aforementioned parish council.

One of these was the never-ending debate about pews in churches. I am/was the Rector of the Taw Valley parishes with seven churches in my remit. Four of them have passionate groups campaigning to remove the pews in their churches so that they can utilise the space more often with plays, social events, bazaars etc. I do intend to put my foot down about the latter, limiting them to church halls only because we really do have to try and lock the door on Mammon somewhere, but otherwise I'm broadly in agreement. Pews are a very Protestant thing—before the Reformation, churches never had them. They never had interminable sermons either which is not, actually, a coincidence.

However, the old-school folk of all four churches are strongly in opposition. It's the Wars of the Roses all over again.

The second matter was about Yoga and, even worse, acupuncture. We have a wonderful community acupuncture clinic locally which offers its services for whatever the local people can afford. They need a new place as their current premises are being sold and they would like to rent space in the church hall in our own village. But acupuncture—like Yoga—is anathema to the dyed-in-the-wool Christian folk. Any alternative medicine is the worst sort of witchcraft and for the Church to condone it, let alone allow it to enter its hallowed spaces, is beyond the pale. What's worse, acupuncture is "heathen rubbish" and Yoga is "Hindu nonsense". No matter that there are persuasive clinical trials on the effectiveness of acupuncture or that Yoga has precious little to do with the worship of any elephant-headed or multi-armed gods, the opposition is powerful and emphatic.

Sometimes I'm surprised this area hasn't re-instituted witch trials.

I've tried using Mammon, as in "we could do with the rental income", to no effect and I've tried "Jesus was a healer and he asked us to follow him" which met with rather huffy comments about Jesus never coming after people with needles or expecting them to stand on one foot for half a day. To be totally honest, we've got no idea what Jesus did with most of his time and most of the assumptions about his missing years—between about the ages of twelve and thirty—have him travelling the world picking up gems of wisdom from other existing traditions. I've always taken issue with those stories because he had everything he needed at home in the Torah but I'm fairly good at listening and nodding when people explain these theories to me, enthusiastically. I'm not quite as good at listening to the people who think that you only have to worship Jesus to get to heaven and don't bother to emulate him for one moment.

This evening, my job was to try and help Lucie make her own mind up about pews and holistic medicine. She swung backwards and forwards, wanting to please everyone and (without realising it) wanting them to make up her mind for her.

I cooked her some supper as I could see that she was really struggling with overwhelm and there was something else that she wanted to talk about, too, but was feeling too nervous to address. This one would have to be teased out of her but I knew I'd better do it before leaving because you don't want to leave your backup feeling vulnerable. She didn't get anything special to eat but there was a frozen lasagne that I had been keeping for when I got back and plenty of time for it to heat through while I plied her with chamomile tea and tried to ask appropriate questions.

In the end, it came tumbling out. She really liked Will and she thought that he might like her a little bit, too, but obviously she couldn't even *think* about it if I objected because Will was *my* friend. Friend, by the way was in inverted commas…

I was delighted. That would be the answer to an unsaid prayer—Will and Lucie! But I had to be tactful because if they did manage to get into any kind of relationship, neither of them must know that I regarded Will as less than perfect in any way or it would certainly backfire on me. I also had to double-check whether Lucie was deluding herself or whether (perish the thought) Will might be using her to get back at me. My ego had a sneaking suspicion that that might be the case.

I defused the issue quite neatly, I thought, by telling her that I wasn't over Paul yet and that even though Will was lovely, I wasn't comfortable with being the older woman anyway. She was free to explore any feelings either of them might have and I gave them my complete blessing. Lucie beamed at me and left on dancing toes at about half past eight. Relieved, I retreated to the living room and treated myself to a final log on the fire before finding my place in my novel. I was at that part of the story where everything had just gone horribly wrong—you know the kind of thing; it happens half an hour before the end of *any* movie and, nowadays, more and more frequently in books. Hopefully I could finish it before I went to bed.

And then the doorbell rang…

As I walked into the hall, to answer it, I lost my balance slightly and, feeling dizzy, had to hold onto the banisters for a moment. I shook my head to clear it and blundered on.

It was Marcus, looking devastatingly handsome and holding a bottle of wine and a bunch of roses.

'I had to come,' he said. 'I know you're going away tomorrow and I wanted to see you again before you left.'

'Is there any reason why you couldn't be with me in Israel?' I said, flattered and amused.

'I guess not,' he said, looking surprised. 'You mean I could come with you?'

I suppose ghosts—especially old ghosts—might be rather naïve about navigating the physical world but I was so glad to see him that it didn't seem worth questioning the ways and means of inter-dimensional travel. I asked him in and allowed him to open the bottle and pour us both a glass of wine.

'It's a lovely surprise but a bit daft to bring me flowers when I'm going away tomorrow,' I said, putting the roses into a vase with some water.

'Don't go, then,' he said. 'Stay here with me.'

He was flirting; there was no doubt about it. And I liked it; I liked it a lot. What (never going to admit it but) middle-aged woman wouldn't like a young, handsome and sexy man flattering her just a little? (Bear with me here; I know what I just said about Will but I never claimed to be consistent, did I?)

We sat and drank a couple of glasses of wine together and talked of inconsequential things. I asked him how he got the flowers and wine and he answered, "from a shop" which, of course, made perfect sense. When I queried whether he found wine pleasant, he laughed and said he was more than familiar with wine and had been for a very long time.

I'm not entirely sure how we ended up in bed or even how I allowed him to seduce me just after I'd told my assistant I wasn't ready for a new relationship—sigh. Yes, he was gorgeous but even so, I should have had a little more decorum. An inner part of me protested as he leant over to kiss me, in the kitchen, then pulled me closer and kissed me again but then my slightly tipsy body responded with a feeling of raw desire. It was so familiar and yet so strange and so utterly tantalising that I didn't object in the slightest when he led me up the stairs. It had been a very, very long time since I'd had sex—and an even longer time considering I couldn't actually remember *ever* having had sex. I know I must have made love with my ex-husband and with Paul, at the very least, but the experience itself was missing from memory. I was excited, tipsy and more than a little confused...

I forgot that Jon might turn up; I forgot about Seraphim; I forgot about everything. I forgot that Marcus was a ghost and that this, even by the furthest stretch of imagination, was impossible.

I'd like to tell you that it was the most magnificent sex ever; that we both were at it like passionate rabbits all night; that we declared undying love for each other and worked out how we could have a relationship between worlds. But I don't remember anything. I don't know if it was any good at all. I only remember waking in the night feeling sick, running to the bathroom and vomiting; wondering blearily what that was all about and going back to bed, relieved that the quietly sizzling lump on the other side hadn't woken up and asked for more. Not quite the end result of passion I might have envisioned.

As I fell asleep, some part of my consciousness heard the distant sound of a dog howling.

I woke, later than I had wanted to—presumably I slept through the alarm. The bed beside me was empty but someone was whistling downstairs. Embarrassed, and astonishingly woozy still, I wrapped myself in my dressing gown and was just hunting for my slippers when the doorbell rang.

Marcus answered it, to my total astonishment, and I heard Lucie's voice raised in shock—not surprising. I heard the murmur of his voice and both anger and pain in hers. Something was definitely very wrong.

I got up, still swaying and went across to the window, just in time to see Lucie climb back into her pink VW Beetle, dashing away tears from her eyes and driving off in a way that would never help anyone believe in the ability of women drivers. The car she cut in front of blared its horn but she took no notice.

I went back to the bed, confused and aware that I had the

beginnings of a migraine. It was affecting my ears, too, as I could still hear that vague sound of howling.

Sounds resumed in the kitchen and I sat, numb and unexpectedly frightened, to see what might happen next.

What happened next was that Will appeared with a tray of tea.

He must have noticed the shock on my face but he ignored it. Instead, he sat down on the bed beside me and said, 'Now, dearest Bella, you belong to me.'

Chapter Nine

I CAUGHT THE bus to the station by the skin of my teeth and the express to Heathrow by even less. As the train rattled through Somerset I sat curled up in a corner seat, sweating from nerves and fighting down nausea. Fortunately, the carriage was fairly empty so I didn't attract too much attention and I wasn't wearing a dog collar so I was just some mad woman; no one important or worth noticing.

I couldn't think straight and I couldn't believe what I might have done—*must* have done—or how I could ever have been fooled in such a way.

It must have been Will. Why did I believe he was Marcus? Why would I see Marcus if it were Will? How could Will pretend to be Marcus? How would Will even *know* about Marcus in order to be able to pretend he *was* Marcus? It was quite, quite impossible.

I couldn't work anything out; the only thing I *did* know was that I had to get away; had to find some space; had to rest and recover so that I could start to find out what on earth was going on.

The blanks about the sex were horrifyingly easy to understand if it actually could be possible that Will would put a date-rape drug in my wine. Nothing else would have made me sleep with him. But why would he do that? Had I missed some clues somewhere? I thought him a decent man, if a tad misguided on the "inappropriate behaviour for a vicar" front. And would I have actually slept with Marcus if I were in my right mind? Sleep with a ghost? And if so, how? But there had been a man in my bed last night and, if I were honest with myself, I knew full well that penetration had taken place.

Yes, of course it would have been more sensible to stay at home and try to sort this out... but would it?

I had been receiving warnings: strong, clear signs from the arils and from Simon the Woodsman. And Alessina and I had agreed that there were demonic forces around and I *knew* that Mrs Tiggy's grandchildren were involved in something. But what? And what could I do without my powers? "My powers!" That was a joke; I had no powers. I was a wreck of delusions with no idea what was true and what was not.

'Dear God,' I prayed. 'I'm sorry; I'm a total mess. Please help me in whatever way I am open to receiving right now.'

It might sound like a strange prayer to you but a lot of the confusion (I think) about God is that we ask for things we simply aren't willing or able to accept because of the mental and emotional blocks we carry. Little and often is my favourite form of prayer. And an apology wasn't needed either, for the kind of God that I believe in, but I was feeling *very* sorry—for myself.

Having offered the prayer, I sighed and straightened myself up to get into meditation mode. That was another thing that Will thought was inappropriate for a vicar but for God's sake! (no, don't go down that road, Bel; don't even think about Will…)

I breathed deeply and evenly and drew my attention into my body, relaxing tensed muscles and letting myself feel heavy in the seat. It would probably take time but I knew that if I focused, I could calm down and listen for what I needed to hear.

'Is this seat taken?' said a very strange, and conversely familiar, voice. It was garbled as though coming down an old telephone line.

I opened my eyes. What appeared to be a wobbly hologram of Jon was bending over me.

'No!' he said sharply as I tried to rise. 'No time! Listen.'

I nodded and sat, my heart simultaneously full and afraid.

Jon's words were short and to the point.

'Rip-off, unstable, parallel universe. Don't go to Israel. Go…'

And then he vanished.

Go to where? What? Why? But oh, oh, *oh* the relief! Jon could still get through to me, even if only just. They would be working on whatever had happened from their side. I wasn't exactly safe but I was safer than I thought I was and Jon would be working on how to get me home.

Rip-off, unstable, parallel universe…

I knew about "ordinary" parallel universes—at least I had heard of them and seen movies about them—but a *rip-off, unstable* one didn't seem at all healthy. It sounded rather like this reality might be the equivalent of a fake Rolex bought on a Hong Kong backstreet.

And if I wasn't going to Israel, where should I go?

I tried to think clearly. One thing about Jon was that he was always precise. The short message had *not* been "don't go to Heathrow" and the implication was that I was to travel elsewhere instead. I had to trust that I would know where at the right time.

The train pulled into Reading which was where I needed to change for the airport. I had half an hour to spare and, fuelled by paranoia, I took as much money as I could from four different cash points on two different cards. Oddly, I seemed to have a lot more money in this Universe, which was temporarily helpful, but carrying more than a thousand pounds in my bag was pretty scary.

However, it's the kind of thing that people on the run seem to do and it seemed sensible not to leave too much of a footprint if I could, CCTV permitting, of course. Probably totally pointless if I'm dealing with pseudo-Celestial energies but you do what you can. With a huge sigh, I threw my mobile phone into a trash can, too. I'm sorry, Planet, I try to recycle but this couldn't wait… It was the second time I'd thrown a phone away; the first was still in the septic tank for reasons I won't go into now. I guessed I could get a burner phone if I needed one.

Heathrow was its usual bustling self. I just had the one cabin-sized case—I'd been planning to go to a hot country, after all—so I was pretty mobile. For a few minutes, I wondered if I should go to the Tel Aviv check-in and say I wasn't travelling or if I should just wander around until I worked out what to do next. I thought I'd go to the chapel and wait for guidance but, almost immediately, I got a powerful urge to check in anyway. So, I did just that, using the automated system, whilst feeling a complete fraud. There was a short queue and I ended up helping an elderly gentleman with his suitcase as he'd never used one of "those new-fangled machines" before. I wondered how long it had been since he went on an aeroplane. He thanked me kindly and introduced himself as Bill Isaacs.

'Amabel,' I said in return.

'How do you do, Annabel,' he replied. As they do.

Hero, in my head, was guiding me. She seemed clearer here than she had been for some time and it was like having a gentle arm around my shoulders, both comforting and strengthening. Once I'd got my boarding pass, she guided me back to a seat quite close to the entrance instead of heading for security.

I didn't sit for long; I'd had more than enough sitting on the train, so I got up and wandered around, still staying close to the departures' entrance and, within ten minutes, I saw Will striding across the forecourt. How the hell had he got here so swiftly? And why? I hid behind a Muslim family with four children and a huge pile of luggage, crouching down as if to check something in my suitcase and peering anxiously around their enormous black Delseys.

Will joined the queue for Tel Aviv. He had just a holdall but he didn't use the quick check-in units, preferring to wait for a human attendant behind a desk. There must be a reason for that. Giving myself brownie points for super-human detective skills, I slid a hand into my case and drew out a dark scarf to wrap around my hair as if I, too, were Muslim. I always carry one if I'm travelling; you never know when you're going to need to respect another faith and it also helps just a little with disguise.

I was wearing a dark, generic anorak and blue jeans so there was nothing particular clothes-wise to identify me and I got as close as I could, mingling with a bunch of students, to see if I could overhear anything as Will got to the desk.

Yes! He was talking: 'Can you tell me if my wife has already checked in—she had to come from a different direction and I'm a bit worried about her.'

He gave my name and, unsuspecting of anything untoward, the flight assistant confirmed that Amabel Ransom had indeed checked in fifteen minutes earlier.

'Oh good,' said Will. 'She does tend to get a little confused. What a relief.'

I slid away, mingling with crowds and thanking God for Jon's message. How Will had got himself on the same flight as me wasn't worth wasting any thought on; he had and that was that. But I wouldn't be on that flight.

However, would they call for me when the gate was about to close?

Yes they would.

I hid myself in the ladies until five minutes before the check-in gate closed, sitting on a closed loo seat behind a locked door and praying every generic prayer I knew to calm me down—and thanking God for keeping me safe so far. Let's face it, anyone who drugs a woman to have sex with her is a rapist and I really, really didn't want to be found by an alleged husband in Heathrow especially as he had already dropped a clue that I was slightly unstable.

'Use that,' whispered Hero and I realised how I could.

Carefully, I slipped out of the ladies and made my way back to the check-in desk. The attendant was just closing down and was about to tell me that I was too late.

'Hello,' I said. 'I need your help please. I've checked in on this flight but I'm not taking it. Can you take me off the system?'

'I'm sorry?' said the woman, raising an eyebrow.

I took a deep breath; 'I'm trying to escape my partner. I'm in an abusive relationship and was trying to get away. But I saw him check in earlier and I'm not getting on that flight. You have to help me, please.'

Our eyes locked. It all depended on the kind of woman she was.

'Do you want me to call the police?' she said.

Reasonable start, I suppose.

'No, it's emotional abuse,' I said. 'Nothing actually shows.' The fear and the stress of the last twelve hours gave me that familiar feeling of prickling behind the eyes and, for once, I let the tears come. I cry beautifully; that's usually a bit of a nuisance as it looks like I'm faking but this time it worked a treat.

'Well, I can call through and tell them you're not coming,' she said. 'I can't give you your money back.'

'That doesn't matter,' I said. 'He knows I'm checked in and he'll keep clear of the gate until the last moment because he knows if I see him, I'll run. I'm just scared that if you call me on the tannoy, he'll know I'm not coming. If he goes to Israel, I've got a better chance of getting away.' I gulped a little. It was genuine.

Eyes locked again. The attendant reached out and touched my hand, which was resting on the top of the console with my boarding pass in it.

'What will you do?' she said.

'I don't know. Go somewhere else. I can't stay here. Give myself time to think,' I gabbled.

Something in the air went "click." I can't explain it any better than that.

'Morocco's nice,' the attendant said, apropos of nothing at all. 'There's a flight to Marrakesh in three hours. You could wait for that.

'I tell you what, Ms Ransom…' she paused and her eyes flickered. 'I'm the gate attendant so if you can let me know your partner's name, once it's closed I can confirm to you that he's on the flight and then you can relax and decide where you want to go or whether you want to go anywhere at all. Will you let me have your mobile number?'

No! said Hero in my head.

And I knew that I'd made a mistake. A *big* mistake. I should have cut and run as soon as I knew Will was there. After all, it would have given me about an hour's start before the tannoy called me.

I hadn't, yet, told the attendant my name but she knew it.

'Oh, how kind,' I said. 'How can I thank you enough?'

'If you write it down for me, I'll call you directly to make sure I've got it correct. Wouldn't want to get it wrong and give you that stress as well,' she said with a slight laugh.

I thought furiously. I didn't have the phone and I'd turned it off before throwing it in the bin so that should be safe. I asked her to wait a moment as I was sure my phone was turned off so she would just get voicemail.

'That's fine,' she said, punching in the number. I heard the echo of my own voice from apologising for being unavailable and smiled brightly as Alicia (that was the name on her tag) said, again, 'that's fine.'

With an equally bright smile, I asked where I could purchase the ticket to Marrakesh, thanked her again and told her I was going to get a coffee.

'You are most welcome,' she said. 'But you haven't told me your partner's name.'

I hadn't, had I?

Bill! whispered Hero. God, I love that angel.

'Bill Isaacs,' I said, adding, in my head, 'Sorry God, Sorry Bill.' But I wasn't giving Will's real name. Belt and braces and all that… If Hero's warning was right and Alicia was going to tell him that I wasn't coming (and paranoia aside, that's what I now truly believed she would do since that strange *click*) then that would buy me some time.

I waited until she had left the ticket console, then shot down the escalator to the tube. I caught the next train into London and, three hours later, I was on a Eurostar to Brussels.

Chapter Ten

My intention was to spend a few days in Brussels and then travel around a little, perhaps go to Paris? Paris *was* calling in some strange way but I felt a bit nervous about that kind of tug in an unstable parallel universe and Brussels is far nicer than people think it is, even if only for the waffles. Everyone should, at least once, sit in the sunshine outside the Cathedral of St. Michael and St. Gudula scoffing a genuine Belgian *gaufre* coated with melted chocolate. You'll need all the napkins they give you at the stall, a bib and an additional damp flannel the size of a tablecloth but no matter what else is happening in life, that stomach-warming sugar-laden gastronomic delight will give you back a few moments of hope.

The winter sun was warm on my shoulders and I felt safe enough for the moment because I knew I still had Hero. Once you know your guardian angel, you can sense them as a guiding hand in your consciousness. It's hard to describe, faint and, as they are incapable of overcoming your free will, very easy to ignore. Hero appreciated my enjoyment of the gaufre which helped me to relax and give it my full attention too.

So far, I'd behaved like some movie heroine whom, we all know, would face incredible challenges and successfully evade her pursuers until that fateful thirty minutes before the end when everything always goes horribly wrong. Some slip of a word, or some random note is found, and her pursuers catch her out just as she begins to hope her life can be transformed. She usually wins out in the end and the opposing forces are revealed or vanquished but then she rarely has to deal with unstable parallel universes and demonic possession and, if she does, she's usually twenty years younger than me and much more attractive. Oh, and in the final twist, the person she trusted turns out to be the baddie and the baddie turns out to be the good guy all along.

I did think that Will was basically good but this *is* a parallel universe and who knows how their movies end?

Once my mouth and fingers were presentable again, I wandered into the cathedral. Its angel was there and, to my delight, I could sense it and it could sense me (why here if not at home? *Nothing* made sense any more). As they so often do, it asked for my strengthening prayers so I knelt as close to the high altar as I could get and prayed for it to be blessed to the full extent it could receive the benediction of the All-Holy One. The angel blossomed, becoming fully golden, tall and graceful. Before, it had been a little faded and dusty. I felt it communing with Hero and experienced an urge to go to the North Transept where the gift shop squats open mouthed to entice you to spend your hard-earned cash. They sell lanterns there in honour of St. Gudula who appears to have done practically nothing in her life apart from being pious and walking to church before dawn carrying a lantern that the devil kept trying to blow out. Every time he managed it, she would pray to God to relight it, which God duly did.

I got the symbolism, heavy-handed though it was, and duly bought myself a lantern, some tea lights and a cigarette lighter.

Our heroine, at this point, would either (a) book herself into a slightly sad hotel using cash and a false name, (b) be helped by a kind stranger which either would or wouldn't be a trap or (c) find her pursuer wandering around the very same cathedral that she was.

Remember, demons are banal. They hide in our trivia; in our 'don't care' or 'can't be bothered' moments and, mostly, just prod a little here and there just to make us slightly worse than we intended to be anyway. So, they tend to stick to the script. Which didn't make it any the less terrifying when a familiar-sounding voice said, 'Hello Bell,' behind me.

My heart sank like a stone. I turned, both hands curling into fists and looked into concerned grey eyes.

It was meant to be Will but it wasn't. Demonic forces can swirl around along timelines and across borders but, I suspect, actual human beings need to be physically moved. And this was a rip-off (and therefore, essentially fake) Universe. The image looked real but if I focused I could see that it looked and sounded like a very slightly blurred copy of Will. This time there wasn't a real human being there on which it could base itself. This was purely a hologram, unlike the previous night.

You probably know already that I have a weird talent of perceiving exactly how people spell names when they speak. It's a seemingly useless talent but spelling is exactly that—all about *spells.* When you name something you place a spell of identity on it, for good or for bad. And when you speak them—or chant them—then you are looking at just that: en*chant*ment.

'I'm not Bell,' I said, sharply. It was true because I'm *Bel* or *Bella.* 'I'm not who you are looking for.' I didn't quite have the Obi Wan Kenobi edge but I gave it my best shot.

'Oh.' The image looked confused and paused as if awaiting further instructions, giving me a moment to break open the tea light packaging, thrust one into the lantern and light it.

The appearance of Will vanished, leaving what looked like a tall thin goblin which slowly dissolved into motes of dust.

Dear God...

Run. This from Hero. I didn't run; everyone knows that someone running in a cathedral is going to draw every kind of attention. Instead, I sauntered back down the nave and out into the gathering dusk.

The gloaming, they call it in Scotland; that never-never time where it isn't quite dark and it isn't quite light. My head was spinning; I knew full well that there is no hiding from either the forces of darkness or the forces of light so it was as pointless my being here in Brussels as it would have been in Israel—or anywhere—but was it? The 'real' Will of this Universe had gone to Israel and it would take them about twenty-four hours to get him back. Therefore, either there would be more fakes, they would wait or they would try another tack.

But to what purpose? What was wanted of me? It wasn't my death; that whatever-it-was could have killed me straight away. Or, if it was my death which was the goal, it was only going to be achieved after some long, slow and nasty psychological torture. That made horrible, if slightly paranoid, sense. The baddies always want to watch you suffer and explain their master plan to you. The good guys just shoot you on sight and get it over with.

'Christ be with me, Christ within me,' I whispered as I walked in no particular direction, pulling my suitcase and beginning to shiver. Yes, I had a jacket and was in jeans and trainers but I'd been expecting to be in warmer climes by now so none of my clothing was prepared for a frosty January night in Brussels.

I'd have to find somewhere to stay; yes, they could find me anywhere but even so...

And then Jesus appeared.

I kid you not. He was a good six foot tall, white, fair haired and, believe it or not, still in that ridiculous Roman toga. He held his hands out to me and smiled lovingly down.

'Worship me,' he said. 'I will keep you safe.'

Seriously? *Seriously?*

I kicked him in the bladder. I took self-defence courses once and that bit had stuck. Obviously, as a vicar, I wouldn't kick anyone in the balls, as all knowledge of genitalia is surgically removed from us at ordination, but the bladder was more than sufficient. The Son sank slowly in the west, braying like a camel.

There was a strange susurration and the world seemed to split in two just as it had at the Bishop's Palace. In one world, I'd made the most embarrassing mistake possible and got to spend that night in jail. In that world the news had a field-day with a story about a vicar kicking an Evangelical who had dressed up as Christ in order to draw people into his church and that, for sure, would be the end of my career. In the other, he *was* a demon and, in his post-braying-ass dissolution, he managed to swirl a kind of smoke around me which brought my skin up in vicious purple hives and softened my bones for life.

Kairos, said Hero and time stood still. I knew I had to make a choice. There were two options in front of me.

I took the third.

Experience has told me that there usually is one—a road less travelled, if you like, and the fastest way to find it is affirmative prayer.

'Christ *within* me, Christ to guide me, Christ to comfort and restore me. *Help!*' I prayed.

Both worlds snapped shut and I was standing in what seemed to be a court room. There was a judge—incredibly old, male and white, hunched in a high seat above me—and two barristers, also both male and white, either side; but no jury.

I pinched myself and it hurt. Okay, what now?

What now, was a trial. In this third world, I was on trial for my life with a prosecutor and a defence attorney pleading their cases with the judge.

The prosecution was vicious. This being knew every moment of my life. I've no idea how long it took in real time but it felt like days as he catalogued every single mistake of my existence; every lie, every moment of contempt or anger, times I was inappropriately irreverent; times I avoided responsibility, handed out blame or was deliberately or carelessly cruel. Every thought, every deed, every aspect was brought out in total isolation; no context, no allowing for any form of weakness. Even the picking of a flower was presented as thoughtless slaughter. It was brutal.

Lucific truth—the truth and nothing but the truth—but not the whole truth.

I stood in a puddle of crimson, bleeding shame, wrapped in the paralysis of terror, hearing all of it. I was a louse; no, lower than a louse—a demonic being myself, utterly worthless. Annihilation would be a blessing. It wasn't nice.

At last, after an eon, the prosecution sat down and the defence barrister stood up to speak. His words, too, were totally unbalanced. Every good thought or good deed was presented; every time I wrote a 'thank you' letter as a child, every time I picked up a piece of litter or bit my tongue on a sharp retort; every moment I listened to someone or was even slightly kind. I was an angel! In the midst of the debilitating fear, I noted that it was so much easier to believe the prosecution than the defence. All of the blame was appropriate. The defence was pie-in-the sky, fluffy nonsense. Someone once said that, to the brain, happiness is like Teflon and misery like Velcro. Now I understood it in my very soul.

It was also no surprise that the defence seemed to speak for a much shorter time than the prosecution.

The barrister stopped and there was silence.

The judge appeared to wake up. He put a black square over his head. Obviously, the verdict was going to be guilty.

'Is there anything you wish to say before I pass sentence,' he said to me and I knew that if I were put to death in this world, I would also die in all the others.

I couldn't think. A deep and powerful fear was biting at my guts.

'*Help!*' I said again. Just '*help! Dear God, help me, please!*'

'Well?' said the judge.

Grrrrrrrrrrrrrrrrrrrrr…

The sound reverberated very, very quietly. And in times of silence, a very faint sound is totally arresting.

It was a growl. And it grew as more voices joined it.

Grrrrrrrrrrrrrrrrrrrrrrrrrrrrrrrrrrrr!

The air around us swirled and then Seraphim was there. The hound, not the choir of angels, but she was as good as a choir of angels! And she was leading the canine equivalent. Seraphim and a pack of hounds… and not just her fellow hounds but the ghosts of all kinds of dogs all racing into this court room to stand at bay around me, teeth bared at judge and barristers.

'This is most irregular,' hissed the judge but he was wobbling.

Seraphim stood right by me and looked up into my eyes. I placed one hand on her head. In this world, I could feel her soft fur.

She barked once and all the dogs attacked the judge and barristers.

For a moment, I was horrified but the men exploded into cloth and sawdust as the dogs bit and tore and shook them to pieces. Then the hounds attacked the fabric of the courtroom, tearing that into confetti which swirled into a kind of bitty fog swirling everywhere. I found it hard to breathe and began to choke. Seraphim took my hand, gently, into her mouth and pulled, indicating that I should go with her. With my other hand over my nose and mouth I walked, trusting blindly that she would lead me to safety.

You're supposed to say that it all went black. It didn't go black; it just stopped and changed.

I was lying on my side in a hospital bed. It was night time and the all-too familiar bleeping of the monitors echoed around the room.

Beside me, Alessina was dozing in a high-backed chair while simultaneously holding my hand—the hand that had rested on Seraphim's head.

Chapter Eleven

I MANAGED TO lift the other hand to my head and touched bandages. Great, another head injury. Just what the vicar ordered. However, my mind—such as it is—and my eyesight seemed clear so probably no lasting damage. Which world was this?

Alessina stirred. I croaked, 'hello' and her eyes snapped open and her hand grasped mine.

'Oh Bel! You're awake. Welcome back.'

Instinctively, I pulled my hand away. You'll forgive me for being suspicious. Battered brain aside, there's been a lot of doppelgänger work going on recently.

'It's okay,' she said. 'It *is* me. The one who spat elderflower champagne with holy water all over Robbie' and she smiled. It was a good smile; wide and generous and genuine.

'Why would you think I thought it wasn't you?' I croaked, cautiously.

'Because you've been on a journey,' she said. 'The doctors put you into an induced coma, to give your brain time to heal, but what is that but simultaneously being absent and holding on? You do live on the wilder side of weird, after all.'

I sighed and tried to turn over onto my back. Ouch. Not a good idea. But my limbs were cramped and aching and now the back of my head hurt too.

'Rip-off, unstable parallel universe,' I muttered, grimacing and trying to sit up but weakness and ridiculous levels of attached tubing prevented me.

'I should probably call the nurse,' said Alessina, 'but she might scare away all these beautiful ghost dogs.'

Then I did sit up; sod the machinery and the aches. At least two tubes fell off and the beeping intensified. Yes, she was right: Seraphim and more than a dozen ghost hounds were in the room.

Not that I could see them clearly but I could perceive the spaces where they were not.

'Oh *thank you*,' I said and felt a spirit wind of wagging tails in return. 'Are you okay to get back?'

Seraphim jumped on the bed and, being a ghost, she didn't disturb anything. Her dear, whisper of a face touched mine—nose to nose—it felt as if she was saying goodbye, her job protecting me completed.

'No, please don't go,' I said, my face crumpling. I felt like a child about to lose a puppy. She kissed me with a lick and turned... into Marcus's arms.

It was the real Marcus; no fantasy rubbish about being in a relationship with a living human; he was here for his hounds because they were his ministry. He nodded to me with a friendly smile and led his charges away down into a swirling (and somewhat smelly) kind of black hole.

'Mmm?' said Alessina. One of the things I love about her is her restfulness. She'll let you know she's willing to listen and willing to wait and willing, also, to hear nothing if you don't wish to speak.

'She's gone,' I said, sadly. 'She saved my life. She and the others. At least, she saved some aspect of my life in that other universe.'

'Will she be back?' said Alessina. Another reason why I love her is that she never says those annoying platitudes like, 'oh she'll be back!'

'I don't think so. She's done what she stayed behind to do.'

'Mmm,' said Alessina again and that 'mmm' had a whole universe of its own: agreement, sadness, acceptance, appreciation, kindness, affection. I could go on...

'Which world am I in?' I asked. Totally stupid question as she couldn't be expected to distinguish between worlds she hadn't visited.

'The one where you saved the Bishop's life by pushing him over when someone threw bricks through his window,' she said. 'That's why you're here. A brick hit you. I'm afraid you're a heroine again.'

'Bugger.'

'Quite.'

I sighed. 'Oh well. Better than the other Universe I was in.'

'Mmm-hmm?'

At that moment, we were interrupted by a nurse who had finally had the time to respond to the annoying bleeping. She bustled in and the next fifteen minutes were a haze of questions, consultations with other nurses, re-setting bleeping things, re-attaching monitors, more questions, saline bag changing and, finally, the oh-so-welcome offer of a cup of tea.

'Would your partner like one too?' the lead nurse asked, presumably having seen Alessina holding my hand (I wasn't to know then that Alessina had been sitting by my bed most days for more than two weeks).

'Yes please,' said Alessina, which in witchy terms means, 'I wouldn't touch hospital tea with a barge pole but if you're planning on making tea, it will give us more time to talk.'

'I'll drink yours,' I said as the nurses left. I was parched.

'You most certainly will!' she replied with a grin. 'Oh, I told them I was your wife; only next-of-kin allowed.'

'I don't think I've got next of kin,' I said, thoughtfully.

'Not *blood* kin, no,' said Alessina. 'Spirit kin. It counts.'

It certainly does.

We talked. Or, rather, I talked and she listened. We switched briefly into everyday subjects when the nurse came back with tea and told Alessina she had to go home as soon as she had drunk hers so I could sleep.

'Five minutes,' said Alessina in a voice far more like Obi Wan Kenobi's than mine had been. The nurse agreed and forgot to come back for half an hour.

It was fairly obvious when the worlds had split—the moment the bricks had come through the bishop's window—but I wasn't entirely certain about the timing of some of the other stuff: yew arils, demonic children, woodsmen and all that. I needed to write out some sort of timeline to get events clear in my head.

'There was a woodsman called Simon,' I said. 'He said to watch out for yew arils as messages. You said you knew him.'

'Hmmm. Can't say I do,' said Alessina. 'So, I was in this parallel universe too?'

'Oh yes. Things had got so weird that you were going to take me on a journey to find out where I might have lost some of my soul.'

'Interesting,' said Alessina. 'These worlds are very similar, aren't they? Yew arils in both and I'm doing my work in both. I suppose that's reassuring.'

'I could do with some reassurance,' I said. 'I don't know how I'm possibly going to face Will in this world.'

'That is a challenge.' Alessina said. 'After all, whatever world you were in, that *happened* and it's hard to discount things that actually have happened.'

'But did it? Was it all a coma-induced illusion?'

'Pretty powerful one if so. I wonder if that world can actually exist without your being there or whether there's another Amabel in it and you melded into her.'

I shivered. 'I don't envy her,' I said. 'It's hard enough believing I'm safe, here.'

'Oh, you're not safe,' said Alessina. 'There *is* a hornet in the hive. And even if Simon the Woodsman doesn't live in this world, there might well be a valuable message that is relevant here. Not all the other world was bad.'

'Bloody quantum,' I grumbled and she laughed.

The nurse returned and Alessina allowed herself to be evicted. Jon didn't show up. To my surprise, I slept.

I was in hospital for another twelve days with both doctors and Occupational Therapists wanting to discover whether my mental acuity was impaired given that I'd had yet another clobbering on the bonce.

'Do you have any confusion about what's real?' the Occupational Therapist asked. 'Any unexpected noises or images—by which I mean are you seeing or hearing things that aren't really there? Has anything about how you live your life changed in any significant way since the first accident?

One of my old bishops had a saying: 'there are lies and there are bandages for the soul.' I'm not sure if I bandaged the OT lady's soul by not owning up to any of that. I am quite sure I lied.

*

I don't suppose anyone really likes hospitals; I know I don't. They can be incredibly hard to sleep in, especially if you are in an admissions ward or tied up to that infernal bleeping. But, even so, there is something incredibly profound about the deep night inside one, with the thinning of the veil between life and death. So many shadows wander. They are not so much the ghosts of those who don't know where to go but the echoes of who they were when they were alive. The souls are gone but some of their everyday essence wafts and mingles until it fades back into the ether whence it came. We are all just recycled starlight, after all.

I could sense them, just slightly, just as I could sense Hero and the over-arching angel of the hospital, and the sleepless parts of the nights were filled with prayers of healing and release for fellow inmates both the living and the dead. People still think that God is some old, white man in the sky but, for me, God is the compassion in the depths of darkness; the Oneness that knows only too well the agony of every kind of crucifixion because It has been there. It is a love so deep it is hard for us to comprehend it but it is there the moment we ask. When someone prays for you, they don't change God; they don't change you; but they do open up the channel between you that may have been clogged by your pain or disbelief. We are spiritual piano tuners for celestial music; the rest is up to you.

On the twelfth day they thought they might let me go home as long as I returned for a load of follow-up cognitive tests. I'd been scanned to buggery and they couldn't find anything they could worry about. I was itching to leave, not least because out of the hospital I might be able to escape all the visitors.

Mrs Tiggy was fine; she just scolded me and fed me home-made shortbread (oh my goodness can that woman make shortbread!); Lucie was effervescent and ditsy as usual and four doctors and three nurses fell in love with her; Will was affectionate and distressed at my coolness. 'I thought we were friends!' he said.

'I'm sorry, Will. I had a really bad dream about you when I was unconscious,' I said. 'I know it wasn't real but it will take me a little time to let go of it.'

'Why? What did I do?'

Should I say, 'you drugged and raped me?' No, he would (as any man would) go defensive and say he would never do such a thing. He might even deny finding me attractive although, for some strange reason, he did. Instead, I fudged something and pretended to be confused. Which got reported back to the Occupational Therapist who wanted me to stay in for an extra day, 'just in case.'

The worst visitor was the new bishop. He had to come as, apparently, the story was in all the papers. Someone had thrown bricks through his window and his celebrity vicar had thrown herself on top of him in order to save his life. It would have seemed churlish not to give the press the chance to picture him visiting her.

Cynical, moi?

'How did you manage to react so fast?' he asked after a good five minutes of politely boring enquiries about each other's health and temper. 'I had no idea what was happening until after we were both on the floor.'

'I don't know. It was just instinct,' was the best, and most accurate answer. 'I saw a yew aril' wasn't going to wash.

'Well, I don't know about you but I've been having some pretty crazy dreams since then,' he said. 'It's all most odd. I thought I saw an angel in the cathedral on Monday. It made me think of you.'

'Why?' I asked cautiously, not sure whether this was a good or a dangerous conversation.

'Because you see angels, don't you?' he said.

Definitely a dangerous conversation.

'No, I don't.' That was the current truth and nothing but the truth but not the whole truth. 'I wish I did. What did it look like?'

He laughed. 'Nothing like all the pictures in the stained glass! More a flickering of dim light. Is that what they look like to you?'

An *extremely* dangerous conversation.

'I'm not clairvoyant,' I said cautiously. 'Sometimes, I think I hear things but I expect it's only intuition.'

'Hear things, like what?'

Okay, something was going on here. Was he genuinely becoming open to the heavenly world or was he trying to catch me out. His eyes seemed clear but 'dim' and 'flickering' didn't resonate well.

'Oh, I don't know, hints, corrections if I'm out of line. That sort of thing.'

'Well, we must talk more about this when you're home and feeling better,' said the man who had objected to anything 'Catholic.'

I made a politely enthusiastic noise and changed the subject, asking how he was settling in.

'Oh, it's all lovely,' he said. 'Such a beautiful county. Everyone is making me feel most welcome. Yes, we must definitely meet up and talk properly.'

Must we? Damn.

I got my discharge papers—or whatever you call them—and a wealth of advice, dates for follow-ups and warnings about taking it easy for a while, and Lucie came to pick me up in her refurbished, pink, VW Beetle which drew almost as many eyes as she did. She announced her arrival with a text stating that she was waiting in the 'men care pack' (main car park). Back home, I imbibed decent tea like a parched camel, insisted that I would be fine on my own and enjoyed a bowl of pasta with a home-made pumpkin, garlic and sun-dried tomato passata from the freezer, in front of the telly. Then I checked that I still had a mobile phone, ignored all the messages, had a long, hot bath with lavender, lemon grass and geranium oils in powdered milk—that way they don't make the bath sticky and the water feels smooth as silk—and got ready for bed.

He came.

Jon came.

It was all right.

We hugged. I sniffled a bit.

He said that he hadn't dared show himself this time at the hospital; they were obviously looking out for anything strange.

'Yes, weren't they?' I said. 'Much more than last time.'

We went back down to the kitchen and talked. No trip to the other world for me tonight, I was still on the recovery list—and there was too much to discuss, from date-rape to yew arils through strange Bruxellianian saints with lanterns to potential demonic infestations.

Oh, it was so good to see him again!

The only problem with staying in this world was that we used this world's time so I didn't get to bed until after two o'clock but I slept like a log and, when I did wake, I threw on sweatshirt and jeans and set off across the churchyard to beautiful St. Raphael's. Nervously, I unlocked the door with its great, black metal key and slipped inside.

The angel was there. It welcomed the flow of love that beamed from my thankful heart and acknowledged me. I felt it dance in another dimension with my own Hero and, joyfully satisfied, I went back home for breakfast.

Right. I was on sick leave, rather than in worse trouble, but that still meant an updated re-working of the session I had had with Lucie in the other world, letting her tell me all that she had been doing, commenting, complimenting and advising. Interesting: if you actually get to live parts of your life over again, like Groundhog Day, you do get the opportunity to be a bit of a smart arse.

'It's like you can see right into my heart!' she said (Lucie is fond of exclamation marks). 'You understand *exactly* how I feel!'

Deja-vu aside, I did. Being a vicar is a huge responsibility even if most people do think you are an irrelevant anachronism with a poncy grade one listed building for hire. Those who do want you tend also to want their own version of God through you and tact and diplomacy about levels of faith are essential. I do, I confess, taper my sermons according to the cut of the congregation on any particular day. There is utterly no point in celebrating the Universal Christ being the blueprint of all creation and only, briefly, manifest in the person of Jesus if the dozen or so people in the Church think it was all a one-off limited edition and might start hurling rocks.

For Lucie, the Work was a slightly baffling combination of all-embracing love and important rules that must never be questioned. Her faith was awe-inspiringly simple: she was in love with Jesus and she stuck with the party line. As long as I remembered that, we were fine.

I'm not in love with Jesus (though I think he rocks); I'm in love with the entire blueprint of creation and I give short shrift to the party line.

I did write down my timeline of events and was sad that the lovely encounter with Marcus, Micki and Seraphim didn't happen in this world. Maybe I met one of the other million Marcuses? Fortunately, I didn't commiserate with Sharon and Frank about the loss of their beloved dog because, in this world, he hadn't died yet… I did look, briefly, at the newspaper reports on the attack on the Bishop's palace and, as you do, sighed at the unflattering photographs of me from the court case that were republished. The bishop, on the other hand, looked magnificent.

I did a lot of reading and resting and, briefly, worried that I couldn't remember when I'd had my last period until I remembered that I'd only had sex in another universe so that was okay.

I was sick a couple of mornings but the doctors had said that might be a possibility during recovery.

And I went to visit the church of St. Mary and St. Gabriel in Stoke Gabriel, in order to walk backwards around the giant 800-year-old yew. Why did I go? I have no idea. It wasn't Hero's idea and it wasn't Jon's or Alessina's either; it just seemed the right thing to do. The right thing for an ordinary citizen, perhaps. The vicar did not wear her dog collar because, well, you'll understand…

Walk ye backward round about me
Seven times round for all to see;
Stumble not and then for certain
One true wish will come to thee.

All the way there, I wondered what to wish. Yes, I know it's an old superstition and I'm supposed to be 'above' all that kind of rot. But it isn't rot; there is so often something at the root of all these ancient rituals and sayings, even if it's only focusing us on what we truly want rather than fussing about what we don't.

In the end, I had to wait for a really long time for the graveyard to be empty as I'm arrogant and anti-social enough not to want to be laughed at or—worse—thought to be some sort of lightweight Pagan-oriented New Ager and I wished (again?) to understand God more. And then, I tripped on the seventh circuit when I thought I heard someone coming towards me, so that probably aborted the whole shebang. It was a young woman and a child come to lay flowers on a grave so I hid. Once they had gone, a dog walker arrived and then another soul come to mourn a loved one. I could have gone on waiting but I decided that a visit to the riverside tea room was a far more attractive option.

There, with an excellent piece of cheesecake, I considered the yew tree and why I had really made this mini-pilgrimage.

It was a female tree so one of the sort that has the scarlet arils. By now, they had all been eaten by birds and the first signs of new, scaly flowers were already showing. I kept an eye out for any roving messenger arils on my reverse walk but saw none.

'Are you there?' I whispered to Hero but she was silent.

Then the activity in the café seemed to slow, just like a clockwork toy winding down. The lady opposite, pouring a second cup of tea from one of those metal teapots that always leaks, became as still as a becalmed sea—as did the brown liquid itself, held paralysed in the air. The waitress balanced on one foot, still lifting a used plate onto her tray. A dog, sitting in the corner, stopped mid-scratch.

I felt a mix of fear and curiosity. I could still move and lift my cup but nothing else here could.

The light became stronger and softer, gentler and colder, damper and silvery and it formulated in a figure next to my table; a figure so tall its head grazed the ceiling and with eyes so bright they blazed.

Gabriel had come to have tea with me.

Not the actual archangel, obviously. Archangels are the energetic size of a star but this was the church of St. Mary and St. Gabriel so its own angel would have the essence of the archangel who spoke to the Virgin Mary all those legendary times ago.

Like a foolish human being, I gestured for it to sit and I'd swear it looked adorably confused for a moment. Then it adjusted its size so that it could communicate more easily with someone as small as me and stood comfortably in the middle of my table. The cheesecake responded by dissolving into a kind of primrose-coloured puddle and the tea, a kind of beige foam.

Some ridiculous thought from the part of my brain I would frequently like to disown said, 'Oy! That was my cheesecake!'

? said the angel and it was a ? that encompassed a dozen simultaneous aspects including 'you believe you *own* this cheesecake?!' together with 'what *is* cheesecake?' and a kind of celestially-exasperated, 'I don't have time for this kind of shit!'

'Sorry,' I said. 'Hello.'

Don't be afraid, said the angel. If you remember, angels don't *chat* so 'hello' back was not going to happen. But 'don't be afraid' was certainly cutting to the chase. That's the most common phrase in the Bible—one for every day of the year—which I'd always found interesting... at least when it wasn't happening to me. In my current, limited, experience it immediately elicited exactly the wrong response: i.e. terror.

I fought it down with some pointless rationalisation—I suppose I do see angels and Gabriel is the angel of this church. And I couldn't go into the church because it was locked. Maybe it thought that I called it? Um. I did think 'are you there?' but that was for Hero. But could it be heard by a church angel? Well, I suppose so, but no, I didn't call. Oh hell, what now?'

Patiently, Gabriel waited for all that confusion to settle; for the over-complicated human to focus.

I took a deep breath and said, 'I'm listening.'

We all know what Gabriel said to Mary but then Mary was a pure woman and I'm not. And I'm certainly not a virgin. So, at least *that* couldn't be it...

Oh yes it could.

'I can't be. I haven't had sex in more than a year,' I said. But of course I had, hadn't I? Just not in this universe and, in my drugged and peri-menopausal state, I'd never once thought about contraception.

Gabriel, patiently, let my tangled thoughts unravel until the shock actually hit me and I froze. Then she (and it did feel like a 'she' but all angels are officially non-binary and are generally referred to as 'he' as 'it' generally seems rude) spoke again.

It is not a miracle. Your body moved to the other level and you were impregnated.

'Oh shit.'

Gabriel considered that remark carefully and did not think it worthy of a response.

'But I … what do I *do*?'

I'm not sure Gabriel was actually expecting, 'Behold the handmaid of the Lord; be it unto me according to thy word' perhaps, but that wasn't going to happen. The situation *was* essentially different after all. That's my excuse and I'm sticking to it.

This is a destiny. You take the third option, said Gabriel very, *very,* clearly in a tone that also said 'you know this already. Why do I have to tell you again?'

Then she was gone. The noise of chatter, of teacups on saucers, of the dog scratching itself, seemed violently loud as the café returned to life. My cheesecake gave a kind of bubbling burp and re-built itself. My tea let off a tiny plume of steam.

I really, *really* had to choose the third option but first, I had to find it.

Chapter Twelve

I have no idea if I have ever been maternal. My ex, Galel, and I didn't have children (and actually, with a lost memory, I did have to check that!) but I don't know whether it was choice or inability on either part. I've no idea if I ever had an abortion or if I took the morning after pill or anything like that either.

But I did know that I didn't want to be pregnant, now, in my mid-forties, from a date rape that hadn't even take place in my own universe. For God's sake, Will had to have been under some serious demonic influence to have behaved like that—what if this turned out to be *Rosemary's Baby*?

Shit, shit, shit, *shit!*

And what the hell—sorry, heaven—would the third option turn out to be? Choosing it, sight unseen had (just) worked in the parallel universe but had it already happened now? Or was it going to come as some kind of shock? Come to think of it, what were the first two options?

I drove home in a haze of anxiety. And, like a six-year-old, ran to Mummy for help. 'Mummy' in this case being Alessina.

She was busy with a client, of course, and Luke was at work so, once again, I sat on her doorstep and pondered life, the universe and everything. No yew arils were involved in this particular time of pondering.

The pale winter sun with its white aureole bathed me in light, the goat willows around the house whispered. Slowly, I began to relax and as I did, I could feel Hero's arms around me. Just knowing you do have a guardian angel is so very helpful. We all have one; we just block them out because society doesn't approve of imaginary friends after the age of about five. I wondered if the tiny cells multiplying inside me had their own guardian angel already.

Yes, said Hero, who would probably know.

'Do demons have guardian angels?'

No.

'Really?'

? Angels don't tell fibs so she was confused. And when angels are confused they tend to back off until their human comes to their senses.

Okay... Thank you.

I felt a smile. I know, angels don't smile but they can transmit the feeling of a smile.

We sat in the sun together, which was comforting.

Go home, whispered Hero.

What? I need to see Alessina.

No. Go home. NOW.

So I did.

On the way I saw Judith Monroe, sitting on the grass verge outside her house and crying. My heart sank but I stopped the car and approached her, cautiously. Sometimes people want support; sometimes they don't. But sitting in front of your house is not hiding away, so I sat down beside her and said nothing.

She accepted the paper tissue I offered, blew her nose with an impressive snort and started to gulp as she tried to speak.

'No, keep crying,' I said. 'You need to cry. There's no need to say anything.'

She nodded and put her hands to her face as sobs that came from her very belly rose up as though to choke her.'

Showing of blood, said Hero. Four weeks.

And I knew what the third option might be. Bloody hell, that was fast! But was that kind of miracle possible? Oh God, please, please yes...

No soul had connected to the tiny fish-like being that had started to grow in Judith's womb and the process of aborting the empty shell had begun.

Was I in time? Yes, it must be. *This* was Gabriel's miracle.

'Here,' I whispered to the little soul that hovered around me, brought forth from another Universe. I heard her giggle and sensed her flow into the etheric of the woman crying by my side.

Not my business, I suppose, how or why this could even happen or how such a blessing could come from such a surreal situation. I thought briefly of crucifixion and resurrection and a flash of concern about that old *Rosemary's Baby* fear but I was simply a conduit here. A conduit for a miracle that I could never speak about but knew was happening on a scruffy grass verge on the edge of a tiny village in Devon.

Judith stopped crying and I knew she had felt something. Hero and her guardian angel were entwined around us both.

'Oh,' she said.

'Maybe it's all right?' I suggested.

'Maybe!' she smiled and stood up. 'Excuse me.' And she walked back through her picket gate and into the house.

Well that's that then. I shall watch with interest. You can't say my life is not interesting.

Mrs Tiggy met me on the doorstep with a litany of complaints: we'd run out of antibacterial cleaner and she wasn't going to use that 'pagan stuff' I'd made up from lemon juice and vinegar. The refuse collectors had dropped rubbish on the verge again which was a disgrace; she didn't know what the world was coming to. And where had I been? I'd been due home two hours ago. Didn't I have a sermon to write? Her mouth ran on, on automatic, but her shrewd little eyes missed nothing. I found myself hustled into the kitchen, instructed to sit down and presented with a cup of tea and a plate of biscuits. I took this all with quiet sense of happiness after a routine visit to the loo where I discovered that my period had started.

'Right,' said Mrs Tiggy watching me dunking a ginger nut, losing half of it, fishing it out with a teaspoon and sighing 'Bel, what is going on please?'

'I don't know,' I said. It was the most honest answer I could give. 'What do you think?'

'What would I know, pray?' Mrs Tiggy drew herself up to her full five feet in that unmistakable gesture of outrageous disdain of the person who secretly has a vast amount they want to say.

'I think you know quite a lot, Mrs Tiggy. And I'd like to hear your take on it. On *everything*.'

Rather to my surprise, she sat down, resting her elbows on the table and rubbing her face with her hands.

'The twins…' she said, her face registering distress that she might actually be about to criticise her own kin to an outsider.

'Yes…?' Vicars are not trained to be good listeners (though we should be). It comes with practice. It was a long time before I stopped trying to finish off people's sentences.

'Well, they're being *odd.*

'And the bishop. He's being odd too.'

'What sort of odd?'

'Their eyes are wrong.' There it was. Spoken so matter-of-factly; just the kind of clarity that Mrs Tiggy was always capable of in the midst of her nagging, chattering persona.

'Yes,' I said. 'I saw that when the twins were last here. And the bishop has it too?'

That was odd; I hadn't spotted anything in his eyes in the hospital. But he had been acting oddly.

'You know what it is?' There was a touch of suspicion in Mrs Tiggy's voice now. Understandably.

'I think so.'

We both sighed. I could see Mrs Tiggy winding up for an denial of what I had just said. *She* was allowed to see something wrong in her grandchildren but it was moot whether I was allowed to.

'It's not their fault,' I added hastily and she subsided.

'Oh,' she said.

'Oh indeed,' I replied.

'They… they…' she gulped.

I waited.

'They hurt a kitten.'

Yes, they would. Or rather, what was possessing them would. I reached out to take her hand. It was shaking. This was a big admission for her to make; that her beloveds had done such a thing.

'Badly?'

She nodded.

'Will it live?'

She shook her head. 'It had to be put to sleep.'

Mrs Tiggy never let anyone hold her hand. She let me hold it. I squeezed it gently.

'What can I do to help?'

'Can you get it out of them, Bel?' she whispered. I could see that she was torn between the need to ask for help and the overcoming of her disbelief about what might be happening.

'You know what I do, then?' I said. I had always hidden the exorcism side from public life.

'Yes,' she whispered again. 'I thought it was ridiculous. I'm sorry.'

'No need. It *is* rather ridiculous,' I said, for some reason. It isn't ridiculous at all; it's just not mainstream vicaring and Mrs Tiggy—and the parish council—are all about mainstream vicaring. Don't frighten the horses with any spiritual or weird shit, just show up wearing the black and white tents on Sundays, help people get hatched, matched and dispatched, smile nicely when spoken to and let them get on with their lives.

'What else has happened?' I said.

'Oh… nothing really,' she lied. I didn't ask more.

'I can't do anything on my own,' I said. 'I'll need Robbie to come over and help.'

'That stick of candyfloss!' scoffed Mrs Tiggy. I suppose Robbie's comb-over caught in the wind *could* be seen as candy floss and he was certainly skinny as a rake.

'Yes, that stick of candyfloss,' I said, gently. 'It's not something one person can do. I'll call him and see when he can come.;

'They're at school in the daytime,' said Mrs Tiggy, in a blinding flash of the utterly obvious.

'Does their mother know?' I said.

'No… she's pretending it didn't happen; that the kitten fell off the windowsill. That her neighbour is just trying to make trouble.'

'Ah.' Human denial is an amazing ability. 'So we would have to find a time when they were with you. Okay. Can you give me as much notice as possible please, so I can contact Robbie?'

'Can't Lucie do it?'

It would eat Lucie for breakfast, I thought.

'She's not trained,' I said. 'You have to be trained. It's complicated.'

'All right,' said Mrs Tiggy. 'This weekend then. Saturday.'
'I'll ask Robbie.'
'He'd better not spread it about!'
'He won't. We don't. It's not the kind of thing you tell people.'
She sniffed and took her hand away with a 'I don't know that got there!' gesture.
'What about the bishop?' I asked gently, thinking *and what about Will?*
'Oh *him!'* Mrs Tiggy's disdain was profound. It was probably partially unconscious wired-in racism. 'He came round while you were out. In his official car. With someone else supposedly important. He said he wanted to thank you again but I thought he wanted to suck the life out of you.'
'Suck the life out of me?'
'Yes. You know…'
I didn't so I just waited.
'He wanted to hurt you. In a way that he would enjoy and that would shame you. I could see it in his face. Oh yes, he was charming and polite but *I could see it in his face.'*
'Okay… and did you find out who the other person was?'
'Oh some church official,' she said dismissively. Mrs Tiggy, like so many of her ilk, was as strong a critic of anything the Church of England did as she was a supporter of good old fashioned tradition, as demonstrated by the Church of England.
We sat for a while in silence with our tea and then both, simultaneously, sighed and began to go about our business again. There was nothing that could be done about the bishop right now; arrangements needed to be made for Saturday and I had Lucie's Sunday sermon to look over.
I don't actually write sermons; I extemporise on what comes to me when I check the Bible readings designated for that particular day. Sometimes the Hebrew and New Testament readings complement each other so it's quite simple and sometimes they seem to have nothing in common whatsoever. However, Lucie (like a proper vicar) agonised and did draft after written draft which she liked me to approve. They were always Biblically-sound, very sweet and—to me—totally uninspired. I sighed, gave

it up, got a home-made wild garlic and walnut pesto out of the freezer and heated it up with pasta. Some comedy on YouTube, a bath and then I sat waiting for Jon.

He breezed in at 10.37 (not that I'd been counting minutes, not at all) and with one look at my face, his own assumed the very expression that he had used every single time he had found me avoiding my homework when I was a child.

'Right,' he said. 'We have a busy night ahead. I'll listen to your problems afterwards, okay? We have a battlefield to clear. Do you remember the Russia-Ukranian war?'

I didn't. I did know that the world order was different from how I remembered it and that Russia was deeply in the world's black books but, like so many matters of international importance, the reasons behind it were a complete blank. That's not necessarily bad; I had completely forgotten about President Trump's existence and, for a while, simply didn't believe it when someone first told me. I guess I was lucky I'd missed it.

Jon filled me in as we wrapped up warm for a trip to the etheric world of the city of Mariupol in the Ukraine.

'Why now, if it happened a few years ago?' I asked. 'Wasn't there a clean-up squad then?'

'Yes,' said Jon. 'But wars are complex. They have echoes. So many people don't realise they are dead and they won't or can't leave. Many are still fighting. You have to give them Earth time to realise.'

Don't shout at me; I don't make the rules. Heck, I don't even understand the rules. I don't like the idea of leaving people in the shadow lands, either, but I'm not currently dead so I don't have a lot of influence in such matters.

As these were earthbound souls, as opposed to shadow souls in what most might call Purgatory, we didn't need to travel through the beauty of the solar system but just over the planet herself, as if in a tiny light aircraft. Even so, as the Panda broke through the clouds, I still gasped at the wonder of the stars above.

'They say that we've observed two whole galaxies for every living human being,' I said. 'That's twelve *billion* galaxies! It's no wonder people can't believe in the kind of God who is solely concerned with what we're doing under the bedclothes and whether we turn up at a small building with a tower at regular intervals.'

'More like a hundred billion,' said Jon. 'Maybe a thousand billion.'

'Wow. With life?'

'Definitely. To quote our favourite author, this is just a small spiral galaxy in a backwater of the Universe.'

'And yet we matter…'

'And yet, we matter. Just as one cell can support or poison a human body, we matter. Hold on! Turbulence!'

The little blue Panda rocked and rolled as we flew into what seemed to be a thick grey cloud with intermittent flashes of lightning echoing through it. The air suddenly felt greasy and I began to cough. Jon handed me a face mask with one hand while grappling with the steering wheel with the other.

'You're still breathing,' he said. 'You'll need that.'

'You don't breathe?'

'Of course not. I'm dead!'

'But your heart beats and I can feel your breath when we hu—*AAAAAGGGHHH!*'

The conversation ceased while the Panda turned turtle and spun in circles. I yelped and snorted instead and braced my hands against the dashboard.

We were going down. It was a controlled fall, in that Jon was still directing the car to some extent at least, but we were definitely going down.

And as we did, I saw rocket fire and a fighter jet. Above me—and then below me—I could see the scarred outline of a bombed city. Hell, it was a city *still* being bombed. We weren't just experience ghostly re-plays, this was happening NOW. And 'hell' was the appropriate word.

Chapter Thirteen

I THINK I screamed. No, I *know* I screamed; I just didn't want to admit to being a wimp. I screamed my head off as we bounced off burning buildings and pieces of shrapnel. Trust me, you would have screamed too.

'Shut up!' said Jon, amiably. 'I can't focus with that racket.'

I shut up. But I had to stuff my curled up fingers in my mouth to stem the flow.

Jon landed the car in what had once been a suburb. You could see the remains of houses and even some left standing but, oh God, the stench. People tend to think of murder and massacre as being without smell, just as it is presented to us on dispassionate screens, but real-life death and destruction stink. Especially at the etheric level where the corruption is emotional and mental as well as physical.

Jon parked the Fiat neatly against a kerb, between the remains of one bombed car and a virtually unharmed one. 'Old habits die hard,' he said, reversing into the space.

I laughed. It was either that or cry. It was a fairly hysterical laugh.

Two humans darted out of the remains of a house towards us. Sam and Callista, my overseers in the afterlife. Two wonderful souls who devote their time to restoring heaven to those who have lost it.

Sam opened the passenger door so I could climb out. Callista greeted Jon with a hug.

'Here,' they both said, handing out helmets and what looked like bullet-proof vests with great golden crosses on them. 'Put these on.'

'Is this for real? I asked, struggling to fit my vest over my head. 'Is this happening now?'

'It is,' said Sam. 'In this version of hell, time is frozen in a loop.

It's our job to get enough people out to break the loop so the healing can start. Here.' He handed me a canvas carry bag which seemed to shimmer and tinkle slightly. I knew it was full of tiny silver spheres that were souls, seeking their etheric bodies.

Here, in the midst of this foul-smelling chaos, I need to stop and explain in case you aren't up to speed with the metaphysics of this story. To be honest, I don't understand it completely but I'll try to make it as clear as I can. Every human (every Being for that matter) has a soul and its soul is eternal—or at least very, *very* long lived. Its body is a one-off and part of a process of helping the soul to grow and evolve. Most of us, down on Earth are fairly young souls, and yes, I am talking about reincarnation even though I am a Christian vicar. I don't actually know if we reincarnate on Earth or elsewhere but it appears, from what everyone who's dead has told me, that we go on to new existences after we die. They may be in levels of the afterlife that we know nothing of, they may be on Earth, they may be on other planets. The end result of all this is that life *is* fair in the end even if the process is a bit of a roller coaster. It's just not necessarily fair in one specific life.

When we die on Earth, our soul draws our etheric life—containing all the experiences we had on our however-many-years journey—to the heavens in order to process our progress. The two are meant to work together in an essential partnership to offer a kind of life review—which I gather is utter, utter hell for those who have been cruel because the ego's justification is the one part of us that is definitely left behind. Only when you have faced your life review and who you really were—as opposed to who you *think* you were—can you move on. Some souls spend centuries or more stuck in the horror of realising, from a place of true clarity, who they thought they were and what they had done. In a glorious, loving, irony, it is the transmuted people they actually harmed who work with them and that makes it even harder, not easier, for the cruel one. The transmuted people have forgiven and moved on and have no problem in trying to help their oppressor. The humiliation of that must be profound.

There is no actual *hell* outside the physical world. There *is* our perception of it. And we all know what it's like to live in hell.

A physical hell was pretty close at hand right here in the Ukraine.

A sudden or violent death can disconnect etheric and soul because the ego doesn't realise that it's dead. People who live firmly in the ego—and that's the majority of us nowadays—have little consciousness that they even *have* a soul and that means that when the call comes to fly, they simply don't hear it.

Other times, they hear the call and refuse to go. If you've seen the movie *Ghost* you'll know that the Patrick Swayze character misses the light and stays behind to help his beloved. In the end, job done, he leaves. But that's a movie. In real afterlife, someone who chooses not to leave can become Earthbound.

Those folk are fairly easy to free up. Worse—far worse—are those who move as far as the shadowlands—grey and hopeless places without soul—and believe they are in simply a continuation of life (you have to wonder what their physical existence was like to believe that and it says much about life on Earth for the neglected and dispossessed) or who do realise they are dead and have no intention of listening to their soul's call or moving on. These edges between life and death is where demons can reside and there are plenty of humans filled with rage and despair and hate who offer an excellent food source *and* a rudimentary consciousness that the demon can use. And that's another form of hell.

But back to the plot… for better or for worse, I was now in a war zone, dressed in body armour which, allegedly, would be recognised as being the equivalent of an afterlife Red Cross medic, and hunting through debris, not for bodies but for ghosts.

Sam paired up with me and Jon went with Callista. 'This is not work you want to do alone,' said Sam.

'Like exorcism?'

'Very like exorcism,' he said grimly. 'Stay very close. There is much here that would distract you away.'

We walked down the residential street. I wasn't sure exactly what to look for and, for some reason, I looked up. What I saw made my jaw drop.

'What's that?' I asked, pointing.

Sam looked, swore and pulled me behind an open gateway,

under the shelter of a sturdy oak tree. I noticed, without noticing, if you see what I mean, that it was in full leaf. So we were not in my own country's season. This wasn't *now.*

'Shhh' mimed Sam, finger to mouth. I shhhd.

Next he did that two finger gesture, pointing at my eyes and then down. I looked down and then, obeying pressure on my shoulders, knelt down, still looking at the ground. It was an overgrown lawn with first drop acorns here and there.

Sam pushed both his and my bags against my stomach and indicated that I should lean over them. Realising he was asking me to cover the soul-spheres with my own energy, I obeyed. Then he bent himself over me and began to hum a deep, sonorous sound that vibrated through my very being, slowing my heartbeat and calming every cell of my body. Until that moment, I hadn't realised how agitated I was.

A shadow passed over us. That was impossible as we were shaded by the tree but, as Alessina said, just because it was impossible didn't mean it didn't happen. The shadow was a feeling—a range of feelings from sulking through despair to abject hatred. And it was seeking light to feed it.

I realised that I had stopped breathing. Truly, my chest and diaphragm were stilled. I couldn't even discern a heartbeat. But I was not choking, I was simply not fully corporeal here—and I suppose I wasn't in any of the levels of the afterlife, really. I'd just never thought like that before. Hadn't Jon said he didn't breathe? So neither Callista nor Sam did, either. After all, why would they?

'Less thinking,' whispered Sam.

Oh.

Carefully, I blanked my mind. It can be done. Regular meditation or parish council meetings both help. Time passed, seemingly a *lot* of time.

'Okay,' said Sam, eventually. 'Safe for the moment.'

'For the moment?'

'Yes, that was an Archon. A kind of demonic angelic thing. They are frequently in war zones, heck, they *cause* war zones. Horrible things.

'Book of Enoch?' I said.

'Dunno,' said Sam. 'They exist. They're vile. They eat souls. That's all I need to know.'

'Like Dementors then?'

'Like what?' Okay, so Sam hadn't been alive during the Harry Potter years.

'Nothing. It doesn't matter.'

'Right. Well, follow me,' said Sam. He held out a hand and I took it. Sam's and Callista's bodies feel cool to touch; Jon's feels as a human body should. I have no idea why and probably neither have they. Sam's hand was big, strong, a workman's hand, slightly calloused-feeling even in the afterlife where there isn't really a lot of heavy lifting. It felt safe to have my hand in his and, suddenly, I remembered my father saying, 'put your little paw in mine, Bella,' when we crossed a road. The memory brought a lump to my throat which surprised me. After all, that was so very long ago.

Knowing me, I could have gone down a rabbit-hole of memories to distract me from the visible, visceral horrors around me as Sam led me round the edges of ruined buildings and across pitted streets. All around us there were ghosts but he seemed to be ignoring them and I certainly didn't know better than he. The ghosts were of soldiers with guns, not civilians, so it felt rather like being inside a horrible, stinking *Call of Duty*.

I sensed a tinkling from within my bag. A soul was calling to its etheric being. It felt almost like a parent calling a child back home at the end of the day, no fear, no anger, no regret, just a loving call.

Sam sensed it too and stopped to look around. The etheric human wasn't hard to find; a little girl in a dust-covered blue coat was sitting on the doorstep of a shattered doorway to what had once been an apartment block. She was holding a knitted rabbit and rocking back and forward, humming to herself.

'No—' said Sam but he was too late. I'd already put my hand into my satchel and the silvery soul rolled into my hand.

As I lifted it out, the sky opened into darkness and the Archon/dementor struck. A huge roll of hatred, fury and hunger all wrapped in one hideous, distorted face enveloped me in a ball of grey. Roaring, surging, endless power pulled so fiercely that my hair truly stood on end and I felt the pavement snap around my feet. I saw my hand crack like shattered plaster as it sucked at the tiny soul. Oh God, the pain…

As I wailed in agony, the other souls, in both my and Sam's bags, began to cry in harmony but where I was amassing pain, they were lifting, turning moaning into singing and lifting and lifting into a hymn of love.

Three voices; one of destruction, one of pain and a choir of pure joy.

It was a battle royal between love and hate. I'd often heard that you cannot fight hate with anger because it simply draws you to its own level but I'd never truly believed you could fight it with love either. But I was wrong.

The silver souls expanded—into me. It felt like a molten river of power and strength, far stronger than the pain and, without a thought, I stood up to my full height and yelled, '*Sod off!*'

Hardly loving, you might say, and hardly original but the joy was power and it was telling me that the only power I had was in my voice. And yes, 'sod off!' was the first thing to come into the vicar's mind. So sue me.

I yelled it and yelled it and yelled it and, as I yelled, I grew taller. The souls were filling me out somehow. The pain in my broken hand was over-written by strength and through the great crescendo, I heard Hero whisper.

Of course! One deep breath and I roared, 'Rus-*El!*'

He was here. Huge, scarlet, armoured, fiercer than an attacking tiger, tumbling in the air with the now screeching Archon. The song of the souls subsided; their work done now that the fallen and risen angels were locked in combat. I became aware that the little girl's soul was still clenched in what was left of my hand.

Without a word, Sam placed his hand under my arm and moved it towards the little girl, who was still humming and rocking on the doorstep as if nothing had happened.

Her soul slipped into her and she smiled and looked up. Her face was Slavic and her nose had a cut on its bridge. Not a pretty little girl but then, to me, the most beautiful girl in the world.

Without acknowledging us or anything else, she stood up and began to potter along the road, trailing her rabbit by its ears so its back legs seemed to dance on the bombed, broken stones of the pavement.

'Shit,' said Sam, grabbing my unhurt hand. 'Where's she going?' And he pulled me along after Viveca—somehow I knew that was her name. She could only have been about five and Sam loomed over her, but in a nice way, covering her with his body. She stopped and smiled at him.

'Can't talk to her,' he muttered. 'No bloody babel fish.'

Douglas Adam's immortal invention that translated every language into the one you spoke yourself wasn't pre-existent in the heavens then? I was surprised. It seemed such a sensible idea. And surely there was something because I knew I'd worked with people of nationalities and natal languages other than mine. But now was not the time to question. The roaring, fighting angels were still crashing around above us and, to be honest, my hand really hurt. The shock, I suppose, had numbed the initial pain but it was crushed and bleeding and its protests were now weaving their way through my mind in pulses that made me fear I might faint.

I'd never been hurt in the heavens before. But then, I should stop calling this place 'the heavens' because it plainly was not.

Viveca trotted on. Sam tried to scoop up her rabbit but his hand went right through it. That was new too; in other places, we were at least semi-corporeal and could touch souls and etherics. Heck, I could touch souls here. Something, somewhere was broken…

Round two corners and we were on the edge of a churchyard with a small, shattered church. It had once had a spire but that lay in pieces across the ground with broken gravestones under and around it. Deep burn marks marked the grass and an old yew tree had been split down the centre and burnt black.

Viveca stopped and began to cry.

Behind us the roaring intensified, there was a terrible and defining *crack* and a snarl of satisfaction. What appeared to be a series of torn red veils floated downwards and across the ruined churchyard.

'Shit,' said Sam, grabbing my elbow and pulling me behind the broken tree trunk.

The Archon roared in triumph. It had destroyed Rus-el, my

protective angel. If I'd had a moment to consider, I would have felt both sad and guilty; I seemed to be a bit of a jinx for protective angels. As it was, I was livid. Terrified, yes, but much, much more livid.

The Archon dived down towards us and, almost instinctively ignoring the pain, I grabbed two broken pieces of yew branch, brandished them upwards as a cross and began to shout the Latin exorcism. I had no holy water; I had no backup; I had sod-all hope, frankly, but I bloody wasn't going to stand there and let it take a little girl, let alone our bags of souls.

'*Exorcizo te, spiritus immunde in nominee Dei, Patris Omnipotentis, et in nominee Jesu Christi filii ejus, Domini et Judicis nostri, et in virtute Spiritus Sancti,*' I yelled. I'll give you the rest in English:

'I exorcise you, unclean spirit in the name of God the Father Almighty and in the name of Jesus Christ, his son, our Lord and judge, and in the power of the Holy Spirit, that thou depart from these creatures of God, Sam, Viveca and Amabel, which our Lord hath designed to call unto his holy temple, that it may be made the temple of the Living God, and that the Holy Spirit may dwell therein. Through the same Christ, our Lord, who shall come to judge the living and the dead, and the World by fire!'

The Archon stopped. Its huge, polluted face stared down at me and I shut my eyes and began the litany again.

And again.

It wasn't strong enough to destroy it but the Archon didn't like it at all. It began a deep howling that assaulted the very air we weren't really breathing. But it had breath—vile, stinking breath which it seemed to be aiming right at me, in a kind of sick imitation of dispensing holy water.

In panic, I lost my temper.

'FUCK OFF!' I screamed, though I knew it was useless. There was no reason on Earth or in Heaven why that should help.

Sam, standing just behind me, whispered, 'How shall we fuck off, O Lord?'

It was like a switch turned on in my head. I saw John Cleese on his knees, asking that question of Graham Chapman in the desert.

And then I was laughing and choking and Sam was laughing and hysteria simply made us laugh the more.

There was a pop. A great echoing screech.

I opened my eyes just as the Archon exploded and ice-cold hail began to rain down upon us.

Laughter and love; laughter and love. That's what it took. Oh Lord!

I fell to my knees. Oh God, my hand hurt. It was dripping blood and the addition of an enormous splinter from the improvised cross didn't exactly help.

I didn't know if we were safe; I didn't know if the Archon would stay dead (or whatever happens to fallen angels); I didn't know if Viveca was okay; all I knew was that if I didn't get help for that hand soon, I was going to lose consciousness.

Sam knelt down beside me and put both arms around me.

'Okay, okay, we'll get you out of here,' he said.

'Thank you,' I said between gritted teeth. 'You saved us.'

'No,' he said, smiling. 'Monty Python saved us.'

Then, God knows how, but Jon and Callista were there. They had a group of children in tow—I didn't notice how many but they were holding hands like in a school crocodile.

'Take Bella home,' said Sam. 'I'll double-up with Callista.'

'Home?' said Jon. 'Hospital, I think.'

He steered me firmly to the blue Panda, just around the corner, opened the door and buckled me in. I couldn't stop making little squeals of pain and I could only just hold the injured hand by the wrist to stop it touching anything.

His face stern, Jon put the car into gear and took off. Any other man would probably have ranted at me or blamed me for something but Jon was not any other man.

Once we were airborne, he reached out and patted my shoulder.

'Soon get that seen to,' he said.

We did an emergency landing outside Exeter's RD&E accident and emergency unit. No one noticed. Part of me wondered if the Panda would get a parking ticket as Jon opened my door, almost lifted me out and guided me through the doors.

I passed out.

Chapter Fourteen

THE FIRST SENSE to return is hearing and, prosaically, it was the words, 'she's coming round' that alerted me that I was back. The second was feeling—and oh, what a relief—no pain! I opened my eyes to two pairs of slightly irritated eyes belonging to two people in nurses' scrubs. I was lying on a trolley in a corridor.

'Are you in pain? What's the matter?' asked one, her tone crisp.

'My hand…' I said, confused. Surely it was obvious?

'What's wrong with it?' Crisp was changing to clipped.

I held up my hurt hand. There was nothing wrong with it whatsoever; the injury had not transmitted itself between worlds.

But that was stupid! If pregnancy could move dimensions, why wouldn't injury?

'Oh,' was all I could say. 'It was hurt.'

'How?' said the taller of the two nurses; an Afro-Caribbean woman with surprisingly pale eyes.

'Crushed,' I stammered, sitting up and examining the hurt hand with the other. Or rather, examining the not-hurt hand with the other also not-hurt hand.

'Oh. Um. It's okay. Sorry,' I said lamely.

'Was that a genuine faint?' asked the woman and her voice was justifiably annoyed now.

'Have you been drinking? Have you taken any drugs?'

'No,' I said. 'No. I'm sorry; it's some kind of misunderstanding. I thought I was hurt. A friend dropped me off…' my voice tailed off. Jeez, this was humiliating.

'There's a head injury,' said the second nurse, a male red-head with a rather challenging and strangely familiar nose. He lifted my hair to uncover the shaved patch with the healing scar.

'Not that new. And an older injury too…' He could see traces of the original scar on virtually the same site.

'Right,' said the first nurse. 'Look at my finger; can you see it clearly?'

I'd swear she was holding up her middle digit while showing me the back of her hand.

'Yes,' I said.

She moved the finger—I was mistaken, it was her index finger—and got me to follow it with my eyes.

I felt like a fraud and she thought I was a fraud—or someone with a mental health problem.

Politely and submissively I tried to answer all her questions while my mind raced. I was in Exeter, a good forty minutes from home with no phone and no money. How would I get back?

Some of the questions were a tad challenging.

'Have you been drinking; have you taken any drugs; have you been in an accident?' were simple enough.

'How did you hurt—or think you hurt—your hand?' required some pretty innovative thinking. I stayed safe with 'I can't really remember; it's all a blur. I think I fell.' I was seeming more and more like a total idiot and becoming rather scared about what they might be thinking about my mental state. Come to think about it, I wasn't that sure about my mental state myself. I could actually understand why people who *were* drunk or somehow out of themselves could get quite angry and shouty at the poor NHS folk who were just trying to do their job. If you simply can't explain what's going on for you, it's hideously frustrating for both sides.

The general view was trending towards concussion which was, at least, logical. And perhaps it had set off something in the brain which should be investigated. But it was hardly an A&E emergency.

At least no one knows who you are, my pride whispered softly.

'You're the vicar,' aren't you?' said the red-headed man suddenly, kickstarting my brain into the realisation that his nose belonged to a family in Thresden, a village in my parish. Pride certainly does come before a fall. But on the other hand, it might help me get me a ride home.

'A vicar?' said the first nurse with that familiar note of atheistic disdain in her voice. 'And wasting our time' hung in the air.

'Yes, said Whatever-his-name-was-O'Connell; his mother was a congregant; I could remember her now. 'She was in the papers, remember? Saved the new bishop when someone threw a brick through his window. It hit her instead.'

'Shame it couldn't get two birds with one stone,' said the woman. Blimey; that was uncalled for!

'Right,' she added. 'I suppose we'd better get her in for triage.'

I sighed. I just wanted to go home.

'I'm okay, really,' I said. 'I've got a psychiatric assessment later in the week because of the head injury. I'll just go home… please?'

'Well, we can't stop you. But I can't advise it,' said the woman.

At least she couldn't stop me. 'Could I borrow your phone to call a taxi?' I asked the red-headed O'Connell. 'I'm sorry, I don't know your given name.'

'Freddie,' he said.

'You can call from reception,' said the woman and strutted off.

Really? I know the NHS is stretched beyond the limit but even so…

'Sorry,' said Freddie. 'She's worked two shifts running.'

'Oh. That's tough.' It *is* tough. Exhausting. I forbore to mention I'd been into hell in the Ukraine and fought an Archon because that had only taken a couple of hours in another dimension. Anyway, it wouldn't have helped.

'If you go round to community support in the oncology area, they might have a vehicle going your way in a couple of hours,' he said. 'A taxi's going to be way over a hundred quid. More, at this time of night.'

Because apart from anything else, it was probably the early hours of the morning. I'd not considered that which meant either that I was completely losing it or… well, there isn't an 'or', is there?

'Oh thank you. Yes, I could do that. But…' I hesitated.

'Yes?'

'Freddie!' came a voice from down the corridor.

'Could you lend me the money for the bus? I'll give it back to your Mum on Sunday.'

'I don't think you should… and I don't have any cash. Look, I've got to go…'

'Yes, of course.'

So, there I was, a confused fool with no money in the middle of the night who had been identified as a confused fool in the middle of the night by the son of a congregant whose middle name was, 'Gossip? Me? Perish the thought. I wasn't the one who started the rumour; I just thought you ought to know.'

Even worse, I had some kind of injury that was, most likely, only going to show up in the heavens which was going to curtail my exploits with Jon somewhat.

I wandered along a couple of hospital corridors trying to seem nonchalant and looking for the signs for oncology and found myself directed to the chapel instead. At least there I could hang out until sunrise.

It was open, thank God. And it had an angel. Well, sort of… I've never seen a more worn-down, exhausted angel in my life.

'I see you,' I said, sitting down in a chair. 'God bless and strengthen you.'

He glowed slightly but was silent. I sighed. I'm sure the chaplaincy staff here were wonderful but no one would have taught them to work with their own angels, let alone angels of the hospital. Not even Catholics remember about angels nowadays and our flying friends are considered New Age, not religious.

So, for the next half-hour, I prayed for and blessed the angel of the chaplaincy and the over-arching angel of the hospital itself. It was bloody hard work and took a lot longer than it should have done because I was feeling tired and confused and cross and humiliated.

There was also some resistance. Not from the angels themselves but from the lost and hurt energies that always circulate in hospitals if they're not consistently blessed. Come to think of it, that counts for everywhere. We all worry about the planet but who actually blesses Her? Perhaps we vicars should all stop berating New Agers and Pagans because they're actually doing quite a lot of our job for us.

At last, the angel raised his wings. That's not really accurate because angels don't actually have wings like birds but that's what it feels like—a great wafting of air or, more accurately, spirit.

And then the ghosts turned up. Hundreds of them; folk who had died in all kinds of circumstances and not found a way through—or not known they were even dead.

The chaplaincy angel looked at me with a query as if to say, 'Do you want to handle this?'

'No,' I said, wearily. 'It's all yours.'

He gathered himself together and began to sing. Softly at first, in a paean of liquid golds, rising in crescendo and matched by others, above, who opened the vortex and began to call their dead ones home.

Oh, it was glorious. Strange to call it life-affirming but it was incredibly so. I felt myself lifted too and strengthened. Colours swirled, song resonated and the room was filled with joy, laughter and completion.

I have no idea how long it all went on but at last I was the only human soul remaining.

? said the angel, while still singing. What he meant was, 'Do you want to go through too?'

'Could I?'

Yes.

Oddly tempting and slightly worrying…

'No, thank you.' I smiled, thinking that the two nurses really didn't need their mad patient to turn up dead in the chapel and, anyway, I wasn't ready.

He acknowledged the response and gently ended the song.

'Hero?' I whispered. At once, I felt the cool breath of her presence.

? I said, meaning, 'How could it be possible for me to go through? I'm not dead, or even dying.'

Your walls are thin,' she replied.

'Too thin?'

Yes.

'What can I do?'

Leave here now. Walls here soft. Both walls loose.

Terrific…

'Hand?' I asked.

Wound there thins walls here, she said. Archon wound serious.

'What do I do?'

Not known. That was the equivalent of 'above my pay grade.'

'Thank you.'

Bless you, she replied. She had never said that before. My guardian angel was concerned. I was pretty sure that meant I should be too.

I got up, bowed to the chaplaincy angel and walked out of the room. Doing so, I stumbled slightly, feeling incredibly tired and slightly wobbly. A cup of tea would have been wonderful but I had no cash or card to pay for it. All I could do was find the oncology unit and see what time their volunteers came in.

I headed for reception. The time now was six AM so I wouldn't have *too* long to wait. Maybe they would let me use their phone and I could wake Lucie up? She, bless her, would jump into her car and come and get me. I'd work out some reason why I was at the hospital though, for the moment, I could think of nothing that would make any kind of sense.

Then things just got weirder. There was a tired-looking woman on reception, probably coming to the end of her shift. I approached her and, just as Hero said, no– she looked up at me and said, 'yes?'

I hesitated. Really, I was just too exhausted to discern clearly or make any kind of decision.

'Um…' I said.

'Are you Annabel Ransom?' the receptionist asked?

'Amabel,' I said automatically.

'There's a car for you,' she said. 'The driver's there. He's been waiting some time.'

'What?'

'There.' The woman turned back to her computer.

'Okay.'

I turned and looked and saw someone I knew slightly. Gerry, the Bishop's driver, who made sure he got everywhere on time and didn't have to worry about parking.

'Reverend Amabel,' he said, standing up. 'His Grace asked me to pick you up. They didn't know where to find you.'

'But how did his Grace know I was here?'

'Can't help you there,' said Gerry with a grin. 'But looks like you could do with a lift. Never seen you looking so knackered! You been visiting folk here?'

'You could say that.'

'Well, let's go then.'

I could feel Hero doing the equivalent of tugging on my sleeve but what other option was there? I was tired, I was weak, I was wobbly. I was being offered a lift home.

No! Hero tugged again.

'We can stop and get a cuppa on the way,' suggested Gerry.

Sold. Sorry guardian angel but I'd practically kill for a cup of tea.

Hero was right, of course, and I knew it but there's only so much you can take before you break. Now I had a headache as well as the tiredness. I followed Gerry through the front doors and down to the car park. The bishop's sleek car was parked close by; not even hospital car parks are rammed full before dawn. Gerry opened the back door for me and I settled onto the smart leather with a sigh.

'MacDonalds or Starbucks?' Gerry was behind the wheel and starting the engine.

'Don't mind. But I don't have any money with me.'

'Not a problem.' He grinned at me over his shoulder and I leant back and closed my eyes.

Ten minutes later, we stopped at the MacDonalds drive-through in Marsh Barton for what was almost certainly going to be one of the worst cups of tea in the world but I didn't care. Gerry bought me an egg McMuffin, too, and I had just bitten into it when the Bishop slipped into the car beside me.

'Well, Reverend Amabel,' he said. 'We meet again. I think we need to have a little talk, don't you?'

I met Gerry's eyes in the mirror. 'Sorry,' they said as he moved the car forward and drove out into the road.

I lifted my tired eyes to the bishop's. Yes, Mrs Tiggy was correct. They were incredibly, horribly wrong.

Chapter Fifteen

'How is your hand?' said a slightly whiney voice from whatever that was possessing Bishop Xavier Morel. The bishop's own voice was gravelly and attractive. Now, his face held the kind of smile that would look appropriate on a James Bond villain. All that was missing was the cat.

'You tell me,' I said, waspishly. 'Who are you, by the way. I don't think we've been introduced.'

That offended it—and I'm calling it 'it' appropriately. This wasn't the man. He would, most likely, be hidden somewhere inside it, either in a kind of suspended animation or—worse—rather enjoying himself. We clerics often have a lot of unacknowledged anger; we have to be, or at least appear to be, *good* no matter how we truly feel. I've felt coils of rage in me at the most ridiculous times when a parishioner assumes one time too many that I will be kind and supportive after six other parishioners have done the same in a very long and tiring day dealing with issues that basically required only a modicum of sense and a teaspoon of gentleness. It's also possible that many of us are co-dependents, addicted to the task of helping others while neglecting our own needs, which means we are consistently knackered. There's growing evidence that some of our current epidemics of horrible, exhausting and pain-filled dis-eases like fibromyalgia are linked to unexpressed pain and anger. I'm pretty sure that demon-possession is, too. The swirls of external negative energy that already exist find a hole in our psyche and dive into it. That's bad enough but even more attractive to the darkness is pride.

One of Jesus's many mind-bending parables warns those of us who think we're 'doing good' that clearing out our own inner murkiness can often lead to self-congratulation—'I've sorted *my* shit!' which can open the door to seven even worse pieces of shit turning up and approving of this lovely 'clean' vacant place to stay.

It's entirely possible that the only reason I've not been possessed (at least I think I haven't) is because I know I'm a mess physically, psychologically and spiritually and that it's only through the Grace of God that I can even keep upright most days.

I'm so much of a mess that I'm sitting in the Bishop's car, knackered, confused and, yes, utterly furious at a sodding demon.

Throwing caution and diplomacy to the winds, I went on.

'What's your name? And don't tell me it's Xavier Morel because even though that's true, it's a Lucific truth and I'm not interested in those. Who are *you?* What is your name?'

The Bishop's mouth opened and a kind of groan came out. *'Legion'* it said. Well, that's Biblically appropriate isn't it? Shame there weren't a load of pigs nearby.

I caught Gerry's eye in the mirror again. He wasn't quite watching the road…

'Gerry,' I said. 'The Bishop is ill. Would you stop the car, please?'

'No!' said my companion. 'Drive.' The voice was harsher now.

Gerry kept driving. I began to pray.

'Our Father, who art in heaven, hallowed be thy name…'

It snarled and then reached out and snatched my allegedly-wounded hand which, foolishly, I hadn't sat on or hidden. I yelped for, as soon as the demon's hand caught mine, it began to crack and bleed again and the pain was intense.

'Listen,' hissed what had been the Bishop. 'You are marked now. You can never go back there with this wound. Stay away from the shadows if you want a life without pain. We are offering you mercy. Agree.' It/they squeezed my hand again and I shrieked and managed to tug it out of that hideous grip. Tears of pain streaked down my cheeks.

'Mercy?' I hissed through gritted teeth and tears of pain. 'A demon offering mercy? Not likely!'

'Yesss. Mercy.'

'That's not mercy. That's blackmail.' I cradled my wounded hand in the other and, to my intense relief, the pain subsided somewhat now it was fully back in this realm.

It smirked. 'As you wish.'

'Our Father…' I began again—and it slapped me.

Gerry did an emergency stop.

'Your Grace!' he remonstrated, as several cars drove past, honking at us loudly.

'… Who art in heaven, hallowed be thy name…*Ow!*'

It slapped me again so that my head shot back and hit the window. Temper thoroughly lost now, I slapped it back with my left, unhurt hand. 'Thy kingdom come! Thy will be done!'

And that was the exact moment that the policemen in the squad car behind us, already alerted by the emergency stop, saw me assaulting my bishop. They turned on the blue flashing light and one of them was at the back door of the car in seconds.

'What's going on?' he said, opening door. Your Grace…?'

The demon pulled back. They may be banal but they're clever, too. It knew that it had done enough and could lurk within the bishop for a while. His eyes cleared.

Xavier Morel, back in charge of himself for now, only knew that I had hit him. He wouldn't have recalled how we got to that situation or even what I was doing in his car.

'She assaulted me,' he said, in what appeared to be genuine shock. 'One of my own vicars assaulted me!'

Oh, that was a very neat trap.

'He… he hit her first. Twice,' said Gerry and I could have kissed him.

'I most certainly did not!' said the bishop.

I didn't say a word, there was no point and I was watching as my hand healed itself again. Oh God, the relief.

'Would you get out of the car, please, Madam,' said the second policeman who had opened the car door on my side.

'Look at her face,' called Gerry (bless him). 'The red mark on her face. He hit her first.'

'I did not,' said the Bishop of Exeter. And who was going to believe me over him?

'What's your name, Madam?' Asked the policeman.

'Amabel Ransom,' I said.

'Ms Ransom, I am arresting you on suspicion of committing

actual bodily harm. You do not have to say anything but it may harm your defence if you do not mention when questioned something which you later rely on in court. Anything you do say may be given in evidence.'

'Fine,' I said. What else was there to say? Apart from 'thank you, Gerry. Thank you very much.'

Several hours later, Lucie came to pick me up. The Bishop told the police he did not want to press charges but that I needed an urgent mental health assessment with a view to being sectioned. In the meantime, I could go home but only if Lucie would agree to stay in the house with me—'for your own safety.'

It wasn't an easy journey home. Part of my mind seemed to have closed down entirely; I couldn't think, I couldn't even start any kind of rational explanation; I couldn't explain how I'd got to the hospital in the early hours of the morning, why I was there in the first place or why I'd slapped a Bishop who was being kind enough to take me home. 'Apparently' someone had phoned the bishop's palace from the hospital because they were 'so very worried' about me—at six in the morning?—and he had come to pick me up out of concern for the mental health of the vicar who had saved his life at the cost of possible brain damage.

QED, you might say.

Lucie chattered about inconsequential things to cover up her own confusion and embarrassment. She finally shut up after I feigned sleep with my head resting against the window of the car. It was uncomfortable but at least it was quiet. I had enough to do, fighting down panic, without having to listen to well-intentioned wittering. She's a lovely woman, far more virtuous and kind than I am—she really is. And she was *so* not what I needed at that moment.

A rather battered Skoda estate was parked on the verge outside my house and, as Lucie pulled up, a human stick insect with a combover climbed out of it. Robbie! Today was Friday and he had driven over from Ely for the session with Mrs Tiggy's grandchildren tomorrow. Oh thank God!

'Bel?' he said. 'I've been here for ages; I was really worried. Your phone's on voicemail.'

'I'm so sorry, Robbie,' I said. 'I'll explain as soon as we're inside. Lucie? Robbie can take care of me; he's staying overnight.'

'Oh, well if you're sure… But no, I promised… I can't break my promise. Oh, I don't know what to do. But I can't break a promise.'

'Come inside,' I said to them both, retrieving the front door key from under a pot plant. I supposed I'd have to find another place for it now, even though neither Rev. Lucie nor Rev. Robbie were entirely likely to ransack the place when I was out.

We went in and, automatically, I picked up the mail and sifted through it while I put the kettle on.

'So, what's going on, then?' Asked Robbie, leaning on the back of one of the kitchen chairs.

'Robbie, they're back,' I said, sitting down with rather a thump at the table. 'Lucie, I'm sorry but it's the same problem as before. When you weren't yourself, remember?'

Dear Lucie, she had tried so very hard to blank out the time she, herself, was possessed. They hadn't been able to get deeply into her, thank goodness, because the absolute worst you could say about Lucie was that she was a bit of a ninny. The best you could say is that she hasn't a nasty bone in her body and she has the heart and soul of an angel. Robbie, on the other hand, had been targeted through a lifetime of unacknowledged resentment about his appearance, his lack of social awareness and his susceptibility to bullies. He was perfectly capable of hitting out in anger and that was where he'd been bitten before.

'Oh.' Lucie sat down at the table and put her head in her hands. 'But you hit the Bishop, Bel. Are you sure it's not *you?*'

'You did *what?*' Robbie's jaw figuratively hit the floor.

'I don't think it's me,' I said, patiently. 'Yes, I did slap him; I admit it and it was very wrong of me. He hit me first but even so, I should know better. Violence is never the answer.'

'No, it isn't,' and 'I can think of a lot of people who would disagree with you on that,' said Lucie and Robbie simultaneously.

'Yes… well.' I opened a packet of chocolate biscuits. 'It's done and it can't be undone. And to answer your question, it could be that I'm possessed, of course, but I can still pray. Usually you can't…'

'Let's pray now,' said Robbie and, while the tea was brewing, we held hands and went for it as if we were rabid evangelicals. Not one of us stuttered or stumbled which was a very good sign and, afterwards, all of us felt better. In this instance C. S. Lewis was right, after all, when he wrote, 'prayer doesn't change God; prayer changes me.'

Even so, Lucie was deeply uncomfortable with the subject matter of our discussion over tea despite the calming influence of Choco-Leibniz and I was itching to send her home just as much as she was itching to go. I *couldn't* tell it all in front of her and I couldn't make much sense without the absolute truth; I would have to trust Robbie with everything and I hoped he'd be able to handle it but talking to Lucie about helping souls in the afterlife would be just too much for her to take.

'Lucie, would you feel willing to go home if I asked Alessina to come and stay over as well?' I asked her. 'I know you promised but it really isn't necessary for all three of you to be here.'

'I suppose so,' she said, hesitantly. 'if you're absolutely sure. I *do* want to help, Amabel.'

'I know you do. And thank you.' I squeezed her hand in gratitude and, after I'd telephoned Alessina and she'd agreed to come over, and then another five minutes of worried dissembling, Lucie left.

'I'll open a bottle,' said Robbie. 'I brought a couple with me.' It was ten minutes before six PM but I wasn't going to protest, especially as Lucie had just sent a text to say she was 'sadly home. Will cull in first think tomato. Take car.'

'There's half a bottle of red in the larder,' I said so we poured ourselves two glasses of a passable supermarket Montepulciano d'Abruzzo and dug ourselves in.

By the time Alessina arrived, I had told Robbie the whole truth about Jon and the other worlds. I know it stretched his credulity to the limit but, as he said, with a sigh, 'two years ago I wouldn't even have believed in actual demons. And even if it *is* all a delusion and you do have a head injury that makes you believe it, it's a good thing to believe.'

'Thank you, I think.' I said. 'I know it's hard to take in—and I wouldn't have told you but that's the only explanation for how I got to the hospital.'

'And yet, there's no mark on your hand at all,' said Robbie. 'May I look?'

I gave him my right hand and he examined it carefully. 'Nope, nothing to see.'

It was so tempting to say, 'you *do* believe me, don't you?' but I bit my lip.

Once the three of us were together, it became more of a council of war. I had to tell the hospital story again, of course, but this time, when Alessina took my hand, in turn, she passed her other hand over it with an incantation and, for a second only, the wounds showed and the pain returned.

'Shit!' said Robbie and I, in unison but for different reasons.

'Sorry,' said Alessina. 'But the Whatever-It-Was is right. That's an etheric wound; it can't be felt or seen here but, there, it will simply get worse.'

'Oh thanks…'

'Jon will know what to do,' said Alessina. 'If it was created there, it can be healed there. Goodness knows how, but there will be a way.'

I wasn't so sure. After all, Jon had taken me straight to an Earthly hospital.

'Will we be able to see Jon?' asked Robbie.

'I don't know,' I said. 'He's never come before if there's someone else here so I don't know if he *can* come tonight. I don't even know what happened to him in Ukraine. Come to think of it, what *did* happen to Ukraine that I had to go there? It seems to be something my memory can't pick up at all.'

The next half hour was the story of the Russian invasion and all the fall-out left behind and I was no longer surprised at the devastation I'd seen nor the amount of people earthbound. Bombing will do that to you.

'But this is incidental,' said Alessina, at last. 'We can't change the past. We need a plan for the future.'

'Well, I suppose we work out what to do for Mrs Tiggy's grandchildren tomorrow and, if possible, find out what they know about the yew arils—and any other kind of possibility of poisoning they might have felt inclined to do—'

'If it was them,' interrupted Alessina.

'If it was them,' I agreed. 'Hope it was, otherwise we have another hunt on our hands. And then, I suppose, see if Jon does, or even can, show up this evening.'

'What's this about yew arils?' Robbie asked, so that was another long discussion about foraging and what is safe to eat and what is not.

It was supper time and that foolishly prompted me to suggest a stir fry with a chicken of the woods I'd found last autumn and put in the freezer. Far too scary for Robbie: 'you want me to eat a frilly toadstool you got off a tree? Nah-uh!' so I baked some salmon pieces in lemon and butter, boiled a couple of rather battered potatoes from the tail end of last year's stock from the garden and made a parsley sauce for frozen broad beans. Alessina ate it politely and it was only when she had finished that I remembered that she is a vegetarian. Never tell me that witches don't have manners… Robbie is a committed omnivore and very much a bachelor who loves to be cooked for. At home he seems to subsist on takeaways and supermarket meal-deals, whereas Alessina and Luke are nearly seventy per cent self-sufficient, never buy anything in plastic if they can possibly avoid it and always cook from scratch. I suppose Robbie and Alessina are simultaneously destroying and healing the planet so I suppose it could be worse. I'm somewhere in the middle as I try my best to live sustainably and sometimes lose the plot and buy a pizza. Then, I guiltily burn any plastic wrapping in the fireplace with an apology to the angels of the air and a prayer that the smoke can be transformed into something useful. Better, in my First World Middle Class view, to take direct responsibility than send the rubbish to Malaysia where the non-stop bonfires of our rubbish make little children's eyes and noses bleed.

Then it was a tea of dried peppermint from the garden for Alessina and me and builder's tea for Robbie as we made our plans and waited for Jon.

Who showed up.

Chapter Sixteen

He rang the doorbell—which was a first. Usually he simply manages to arrive while I'm not looking or, quite frequently, while I'm still in the bath.

'Wait here,' I said to Robbie and Alessina. 'If I call out, then it isn't Jon. If I don't, then give me some space, please.'

'Okay.' Alessina was relaxed and Robbie looked relieved that I didn't want him to answer the door for me, in case it was (a) a ghost or (b) a possessed Bishop.

'How did you know to come when I'd got company?' I asked. He didn't give me an answer other than his normal, 'still focusing on the "hows" Bel? It's ineffable, remember?' And then he shot himself in the virtual foot by asking, 'how is your hand?'

'Still focusing on the "hows" Jon?' I replied with massive wit which didn't quite go down like a lead balloon but certainly scuttled away down a mouse hole, riddled with its own embarrassment at one apposite raised eyebrow.

Jon sighed. Or, more accurately, his being dead and all that, he appeared to sigh.

I sighed for real and suggested we sat down on the front porch to catch up before I tried to introduce him to Alessina and Robbie.

'This is all my fault,' said Jon, after I'd told him the whole assaulting-the-Bishop story. 'I never even considered that your wound wouldn't be earthly. Stupid of me. If I hadn't delivered you to the hospital, this wouldn't have happened.'

'Well, it is what it is,' I said. 'I suppose we all panicked.'

'Hmmm. Well, I suppose we do have to try and see if the Bishop's demon was lying or not. They do lie very well.'

'It would make some sense though—that a wound received on another level would still exist on that level even if it didn't carry through. But can it be healed on that level?'

'I'm sure it can,' said Jon. 'The question is...' he stopped.

'The question is...?'

'I was going to say "how"' he said with a grin. 'Maybe I need to go out and come back in again.'

We sat together for a short while, looking up at the stars. I live on a road with no street lights on the edge of a tiny village overlooked by the Milky Way which streams overhead like a river to the heavens. When you've driven through it in an ancient blue Fiat Panda, it becomes even more special.

'Why do you want your friends to see me?' he asked eventually. 'And don't say, "so they'll believe what I told them."'

It was a good question. And one I couldn't answer immediately.

'Yes, there's that,' I admitted after a minute. 'And, I suppose, to explain about why I was at the hospital in the first place.'

'You could have thought up something a little more feasible!' said Jon.

'No, I couldn't. The Bishop-demon's ruse seems to be to make me look incompetent and even mentally ill and I don't want them even thinking about that.'

'So it's all about you?'

'Yes.'

'Okay.'

Sometimes, even now, Jon is still a big brother and I'm an exasperating little sister.

He put his arm around me.

'They won't see me,' he said. 'In your world, you'd call it an algorithm. I'm not written into their programming like I am written into yours.'

'Not even as a ghost?'

'I'm not a ghost,' said the perfectly dead man sitting by my side.

'What shall we do, then?' I asked.

'Perhaps I need to go back without you,' said Jon. 'And find out who can help.'

We both sighed.

'Did Sam and Callista get the people through?' I asked.

'No. There wasn't a portal. The Archons had closed it.'

'Archons plural?'

'Yes.'

'Do you actually mean the fallen Powers and Principalities of the archangelic realms? That there really *is* war in heaven?'

'I'm afraid so. And it's a lot worse now humanity has chosen entropy. The effect in the imaginal realm is drawing the darkness closer.'

'The what realm?'

'Imaginal. Didn't you read that Gurdjieff I left you?'

'I tried Ouspensky but he beat me.'

Jon laughed. 'Shame. Oh well. The Imaginal Realm is where human thought and belief meld with the spiritual level in a kind of mutual feeding. When humanity is mired in apathy, entropy and distraction, the field becomes heavy and stagnates. That attracts darker beings.'

'Hang on—you mean *we* have an effect on what happens in the heavens?'

'So asks the vicar who lives a life in prayer!'

'I meant all of us, whether we believe anything or not.'

'Yes. It's a bit complicated but when humanity reaches up in consciousness, seeking the good while also allowing itself simultaneously to experience the grief of the world, without judgment or hatred, it feeds a form of clear energy into spirit. When humanity distracts itself from those feelings with the latest television series where it can hide its anger in murder mysteries and super-hero battles, then it sends the energy of those very shows into spirit by default.'

'The super heroes and the detectives do win,' I said, defending my species rather desperately.

'At what cost?' asked Jon. 'As soon as you fight something negative, you lower your energy to the level of your enemy. Fighting never enhances spirit. The cycle of life is that everything provides food for everything else. You see that in nature, yes?'

'Yes.'

'But humanity really doesn't feed anything back. You don't even bury the majority of your dead to give back nutrients to the Earth. So, humanity's job is to feed spirit with consciousness.'

'*Really?*'

'It's the simplest way of explaining it. It's how this solar system works, at least. You do know the Gospel of Thomas, right?'

'Yes,' I said. 'Well, I've read it,' I added, reluctantly. I didn't remember much.

'Blessed is the lion whom the man devours, for that lion shall become man. But cursed is the man whom the lion devours, for that man shall become lion,' quoted Jon.

I brightened up. 'Yes, I *do* recall that bit. So, if we overcome our animal instincts then we can feed spirit with good humanity. But if we allow our animal instincts to overcome us, we feed spirit with anger or worse. But, hang on—lions aren't angry; they just feed on what they need.'

'Indeed they do. It is indeed a metaphor. What do the majority of humans feed on—and do humans only feed on what they need?'

'No, we eat rubbish food in takeaways and blog in front of movies and TV to distract ourselves.'

Guilty as charged, I thought…

'Exactly. And the more humanity does that, the more negative, lazy, entropic and uncaring energy they transmit into spirit. And spirit has to eat it.'

'But hang on, there have been wars since the start of time and we've only had TV and movies for a hundred and fifty years.'

'It's only just beginning to show,' said Jon. 'The heavens have been able to cope with most of it all up until now. With some seriously bad breakthroughs like the Crusades, the Inquisition, a couple of world wars and the Holocaust. But it's getting critical now; the tipping point was the worldwide pandemic of Covid-19. The Archons are breaking through to the etheric. That's why we need the help of people like you who have spanned the worlds of life and death.'

'Gurdjieff said human entropy feeds the moon while human consciousness feeds the Earth,' said a gentle voice behind us..

Jon stood up and bowed to her. Alessina bowed back.

'Yes. The moon representing illusion, something which appears to shine but is only a reflection,' Jon said. 'So you are feeding illusion, feeding a dead thing which controls the waters—the emotions—instead of feeding the planet you live on.'

'You can see him?' This was Rev. Amabel Ransom voicing a blinding flash of the bleedin' obvious.

'I can both hear and perceive him,' said Alessina, smiling. 'I can't *see* him. Nevertheless, I am glad to meet you, Sir.'

'And I you, Madam,' replied Jon. 'I am impressed!'

'So,' said Alessina, honouring the compliment with a nod. 'We are feeding fallen angels through our obsession with distracting ourselves from our troubles instead of working to resolve them.'

'In a nutshell, yes,' said Jon. 'Ironically, all humanity needed to do to hold the balance was to take a weekly Sabbath from all the images of violence. Now, only the ultra-orthodox do that in any religion and they aren't all filled with creative, inclusive energy…'

'The Sabbath was made for humanity, not humanity for the Sabbath,' I quoted.

'Kind of—but actually the Earth needs the Sabbath too,' said Jon. 'Humanity may not have been created for the Sabbath but we were created to live in harmony with our planet and its solar system.'

My phone went 'ping' in my pocket. Automatically, I took it out and looked at the text. It was Lucie checking that I was all right, or, as her auto-cucumber typed it, 'R U OK? Did you cock someone toasty for supper?' I snorted.

'Shortened attention spans aren't helping either,' said Jon, wryly.

'No, but humour does,' I said, showing them both the text.

'Cock someone toasty?' said Jon who, you'll remember, died long before mobile phones ruled the world.

'Cook something tasty,' I said. 'It's a programme that's meant to correct your spelling but it mostly goes rogue. Lucie never checks before she sends. She sent me one on Easter morning last year, exclaiming "Gory be: Chris has raisins!"'

Jon just stared at me.

'Sorry,' I said. 'It's polite to reply. I won't be a minute.'

I texted back. 'yes thanks' and put the phone away.

'Where were we?' I asked.

'Proving a point,' said my big brother.

'Is it worth finding out if it's actually true that Bel can't go to the higher realms because of her hand?' asked Alessina. 'I know I've sensed the wound and we believe what the bishop told her but…'

'It's up to her,' said Jon. 'Bel, are you up for trying now? I can bring you back pretty fast. And, if it is okay, Sam and Callista could do with more help. We don't know if it was simply not having a living-dead human with us that stopped the souls going through.'

'Okay,' I said, slightly doubtfully. 'But can I shout "stop" the moment it starts hurting?'

'Of course,' said Jon, standing up. 'Well then…'

'How long will you be?' asked Alessina.

'About five minutes of your time,' said Jon. 'Shorter if possible.'

'Then I'll wait with Robbie.' Alessina nodded to Jon and turned back into the hall.

'She's amazing,' I said.

'She most certainly is. Okay, are you sure you want to do this?'

'I don't know! Yes, I think so.' I paused; Hero was whispering in my ear. 'Hang on, Jon…

Okay, can you make sure you bring me back right here—or even closer to the church if possible? It *is* St. Raphael's after all and it does have its own angel. She once told me she could heal.'

'Sure,' said Jon. 'So, all your congregation are healthy then?'

'I wish…' But he'd got me thinking. Why didn't I see if there was a healing service we could run? Ariel was 'of Raphael' so surely some good could be done. Why had I never thought of this before?

'Could you wait a few more minutes while I go into the church and ask?'

'I've got all the time in the world,' said Jon, accurately. 'But we did tell Alessina we would be back in a few minutes.'

'I'll run.' It only took a moment to pick up the torch and the side key to the vestry from the key rack by the front door and I trotted off to St. Raphael's with Jon walking behind. The old

Norman church was eerily beautiful at night time with a waning gibbous moon creating silvery shadows through the ancient stained glass over the altar.

Ariel was there and expecting me. I don't know how angels communicate but I like to think that she and Hero probably hang out at some kind of cosmic Starbucks swapping stupid human stories…

'And then she did *this!*'

'No!'

'Oh yes she did.'

'What a plonker!'

'I did try and warn her.'

'Of course you did, but they never bloody listen, do they?'

It's no wonder the discarnate are called 'spirits'; they probably need celestial vodka to cope.

'Healing? Healing services?' I thought to her.

Yes!' Ariel brightened and grew. I perceive her normally as being about six feet tall and one foot wide but now she seemed half as big again.

'And heal my hand?'

Ariel scanned me carefully. Her attention focused in my right arm and hand and I felt a wild and visceral tingling. She flinched and shrank back to her normal size.

'That's not good,' I thought, as a sound like keening broke into my consciousness; it was both Ariel and Hero.

I was aware that both of them knew the origin of the invisible wounds and also that neither of them would articulate it because their words would give power and that power could draw the darkness. I can't tell you *how* I knew that, but I did. I suppose it was ineffable.

The song, or cry, grew… and grew… and grew and then a great shaft of cadmium yellow light formed over the altar and another song joined in harmony. Something was coming; something vast and powerful and magnificent.

I found myself falling face down on the floor as an emissary of the great Archangel Raphael emerged into this space-time. It was far too big for the church but seemed to be able to compress itself to fit. The very stones of St. Raphael's groaned as astral life-force filled them. If the church could have sprouted leaves or flowers, it would have. It pulsed with *essence*.

This wasn't the whole of Raphael—an archangel is energetically the size of a star, remember?—but it was awe-inspiring enough for the hairs on my head to stand up and for tears of joy to form in my eyes. I couldn't have got up to save my life; my legs were junket.

Jon, emerging from the vestry, knelt on one knee beside me.

'Lord,' he said, bowing his head.

Human, said the Presence, in acknowledgment. It bowed what might have been a head in return.

Jon nudged me with his foot.

'Sir,' I stuttered.

Human, replied the Presence again. A stream of light flowed from it to me, encouraging me to stagger onto jellified legs and wobble before it. I could feel this wonder of Creation's querying as to why it had been called. It knew it was here on my behalf but until I made my request, no further communication would ensue.

I looked at Jon for help. 'It has to be you,' he said. 'Just speak but don't mention the A-word.'

'My hand,' I stuttered, holding it up. 'Damaged by… by a fallen one in etheric Ukraine. Please will you heal it?'

Another scan. This one felt as though my blood had been replaced by champagne in a bottle deliberately shaken. I fell over. Well done, Bel. Nothing like a bit of elegance, is there?

I felt kindness; I felt hope; I felt quicksilver replacing the champagne in my arteries. I felt hot and cold and curious and clear.

We will, said the angel. Return to Ukraine. We shall meet you there.

It didn't fade and yet there was a softness to its vanishing. If there hadn't been, I would have wept with grief at the loss. Certainly the church was dark and cold and lonely without it. The stones sighed, creaked and re-settled into their ancient places and Ariel seemed strangely washed out.

'Okay, let's go,' said Jon, brusquely.

*

An Archon was waiting for us.

'Shit!' spat Jon, hauling at the steering wheel as it rose up in front of the Panda the moment we began our descent into Mariupol. The Fiat turned turtle and skidded—if you can skid in air—like a tennis ball smashed by a racquet on ice. No, it's not a very good simile but it will have to do in the heat of the moment.

The traditional phrases at such a time would be either 'I can't hold her!' or 'She's going down!' But, as this wasn't a movie, both of us just screamed, 'FUUUCCCCKKKKK!'

Somehow, we landed on one wheel, then two wheels and then four and slammed to a stop by hitting the remains of a bus stop.

For long seconds, nothing happened. We looked at each other, wordlessly, then both peered upwards out of the windows.

'Jesus,' whispered Jon. 'There *is* war in heaven.'

We'd heard of that, of course—Revelation, chapter twelve. Now it was happening before our very eyes and without the help of the magic mushrooms on Patmos.

Angels and Archons, both in fantastic, indescribable forms, not remotely human, seemed to be crashing and smashing at each other. Firebolts, thunderbolts, colours that screeched, sounds that stank, smells that blinded, folded and unfolded, strafed the skies. Everything shuddered and the noise was soul-splitting.

But before we could take a second glance, Sam and Callista were opening the car doors and pulling us out. 'Quick!' they shouted, pulling us into a still-partially-standing building. We staggered in over rubble and found ourselves inside the remains of a church, its nave and pews filled with children, women and old folk. My heart contracted at the sight of them; dead and yet still wounded; still suffering. All of them were greyed out through pain and grief and the lack of light that the earthbound dead must live in seemed to be gnawing at their etheric bones. It was a place which should have been resonant with faith, mired in hopelessness.

'We can't get them through,' said Sam. 'There's no path. Can you help? A living human might help...'

I opened my mouth to speak but my voice caught in my throat as shears of pain cut into my wounded hand, slashing it open so that blood began to flow again.

'Bugger,' said Jon, pulling out a big white handkerchief. Those were so much a part of my childhood—'Tissues? Rubbish!' that there was an astonishing comfort that almost swallowed the pain as he bandaged the hand as well as he could.

'Apply pressure,' he said, tying a knot. 'Hold it as hard as you can. That should ease the flow. Do you want me to take you straight back?'

'No,' I muttered through gritted teeth. I bent over myself, cradling the wounded hand in the other and doing what I could to ease it. And I cursed to myself; what use could I be here? And why had we been sent back if there was nothing to help me here?

'You selfish cow,' I thought. 'You've been sent for a *reason*. You *know* that. There *must* be a reason. But what the hell *is* it?'

One of the children came up to me. It was the same little girl whom Jon and I had tried to help before in the dust-covered blue coat and carrying her much-loved knitted rabbit. She held out the rabbit to me, silently and, as I smiled at her, I noticed that the rabbit had a red carrot in its paws. Red… red… red arils. I remembered! This could be the stupidest suggestion I could make but, at that moment, it seemed ridiculously clear.

'Yew!' I ejaculated. 'Have you tried a living yew? There was one in the churchyard Viveca led us to before but it was dead. A living one might do it.'

'What?' said Sam.

'Yew trees! Legend says they were the places where souls could get through. That's why they were planted in churchyards. Can we find a living yew?'

'I thought they repelled demons,' said Callista.

'Might be both,' said Sam. 'Worth a try.'

Yes, said Hero, softly in my ear. Follow.

And for the first time, I *saw* my guardian angel. Maybe the pain was clearing my senses in some odd way—and that was definitely a first—but I could see a silvery-blue form, etheric and exquisite and very nearly humanoid holding out a hand to me.

And I could see Jon's guardian too. And Sam's. And Callista's. They were shining.

'Can you see them?' I asked.

'Of course,' they all said with slightly grim smiles. I suppose, in the heavens, you do. But that would have to wait.

'Follow us,' I said, letting Hero guide me.

We left in one long crocodile, keeping in shelter as much as we could while the explosions continued above. I hardly registered them; all my attention was on being able to walk without yelping; every footfall jarring my bleeding hand. Hero indicated that she wished she could sing comfort to me but silence was vital at this moment. I'd seen what an Archon could do to an angel so I could see her point.

Of course, I had assumed that other countries had yew trees in their graveyards but if they didn't have druids, why would they have yew? It wasn't the Christians who had started this magical relationship.

We passed two shattered churches with no graveyard at all and another still standing with no yew tree. Hero indicated onwards and upwards. I was stumped.

It seemed like a very long time before we reached what had been the gates to Mariupol's equivalent to a botanical gardens. And there, gnarled and worryingly small, was just one yew.

It had lost nearly half its branches in the bombings but those that remained still held life.

Pocket, said Hero. I put my hand in my right pocket and, against all the odds, came out with one squashed aril on my finger. A light seemed to extend from it to the tree which began to vibrate.

'Yes!' said Callista. 'I can see the vortex! Can you?'

And I could; the deva of the tree itself was coming out to greet us. A strange and gnarly creature, more like a troll than a spirit, it shimmered with a faint but growing light both within and outside of the tree, encompassing it in a deep green softness and what looked, to my prosaic eyes, like a door opened inside her etheric body.

'Quick!' said Sam, ushering the little girl in the blue coat towards the light that flowed softly from the deva's heart space. She hesitated and then ran forward. I thought I saw someone come towards her from another world inside the trees and she cried out, 'Mumiya!'

Then she was gone.

Swiftly, Sam and Callista guided the next dozen people forward and through and then there was a bellow of fury and an Archon slammed into the tree and its Deva, shattering them into a thousand pieces.

Chapter Seventeen

It heaved itself up, emitting a cross between a roar and a groan and stood (if that's the right word) about nine feet tall before me. So, it was a pretty small Archon, really, like a pretty small great white shark.

For some reason, as the others, behind and beside me, seemed to fade away, I stepped forward. It wasn't bravery—or even stupidity—it just was what I knew I had to do. I'd done it before with both sharks and demons and both times it had worked.

Hero moved forward beside me and whispered, trust.'

And it destroyed her with one shaft of dark light that shattered her like water drops from a cobweb. Just as it had shattered the Deva.

Time passes differently in a crisis and slowly, slowly, over less than half a second, I felt life-force drain away from me. Without Hero I was more than naked; I was incomplete and inarticulate and no longer quite *me.*

I suppose I'm about to die, I thought, without emotion.

Then make it worth it! Came an unidentifiable voice and I felt my fists ball up. As if I, a puny human, could do anything here.

You could laugh, came what was definitely a memory but underneath it was a much more powerful impulse. My brain thought, 'that's impossible!' yet I obeyed and stepped forward, again, holding my arms out.

'I love you; I'm sorry, please forgive me. Thank you,' I said to the dark angel and walked straight into it.

He walked with me and, together, we explored this strange grey world. It was *huge.* Inside the Archon was everything it had swallowed since the moment of its creation. None of it was dead; all of it was suffering and that anguish fuelled the angel. There were acres of rage and grief; oceans of fury and despair; volcanoes of savagery and hate. There was also a heartbeat or, at least, a kind of pulse.

He took my hand, the wounded one. I screamed and staggered and then the pain was gone. 'There,' He said, gently, 'all done.'

'Why are you here?' I asked.

'You called.'

'I didn't!'

'Yes, you called Love. Not a persona.'

'Ah.' Love. Yes, of course…

'So use me,' He said. And, slowly, hesitantly, inarticulately and to devastating effect, I began to think thoughts of love. I blessed the Archon—and all Archons. I drew up every memory of everyone I could think of whom I had ever hated or raged against and blessed them. I drew on all the experiences of love that I contained and He magnified them, added to them, depleted any manipulation or dis-ease from them and wove them in and around me and through me into the pulse of the angel.

Oh my God, it was cruel. Hideously cruel. Because every bead of love tortured it. I shivered as I felt its pain and deep compassion gripped me.

'Stop!' I said to Him.

'No,' he said, gently. 'It must be. Did it not hurt when I healed your hand? *This is the only hell there is; the refusal to love and be loved.* She can surrender at any time.'

'She? Oh poor love…'

I don't know why giving a gender to the Archon broke my heart but it made her more real, I suppose. And while my brain could register disbelief that I was aching with compassion for a murdering bundle of pure evil, my soul could only open wider and offer more of itself.

She did fight back and she was cunning.

Out of the blue came the memory of a fellow vicar who kept quoting 'Shakespeare's "hell hath no fury like a woman scorned,"' and that very woman was standing before me in this moment saying it again. I could anticipate my shadow correcting her, saying, 'Actually, it's not. It's from William Congreve's play, *The Mourning Bride*, written in 1697. The line from which it came is "Heaven has no rage like love to hatred turned, nor hell a fury like a woman scorned."'

And I managed not to say it! My God, it was hard but I did it.

The Archon offered more and more of the same; all the times I had contradicted people, criticised people, patronised people (and there were *so* very many of them) and, with my little paw held safely in His hand, I blessed and blessed and forgave and asked for forgiveness and loved and loved and loved.

Eventually, there was no time; there was no noise, no darkness; nothing but space and light and love—and that pulse. With a soft sigh, the Archon dissolved into a small, delicate fairy-like creature, about the size of my formerly-wounded hand.

He picked her up and spoke to her and together they shared a moment of profound sorrow and understanding and then she flew away in a trail of motes of light like stardust.

'Here,' He said, indicating a wooden bench that had materialised out of nowhere. 'Let us sit.'

That made me chuckle; it was so like 'let us pray.'

I sat.

'So, ask!' He said with a smile. 'Anything.'

Guess what? You forget your questions when this kind of thing happens. Well, most of them, anyway.

'Why me? I'm not worthy.' (that's it, Bel, make it all about you. You could ask about *anything* and you make it about you).

He laughed.

'You're right,' He said. 'You're not "worthy." You'll probably never be "worthy" but who cares about worthy? You listen. The listeners are what we need. Nobody is "worthy", particularly those who think they are.'

'Oh.' That was Christianity—and most other religions too—totally out of the window. I'm not a fan of the word 'empowered' but that's how I felt. A huge weight I never knew I was carrying fell from my shoulders. It was glorious.

'We?' I asked, tentatively.

'Yes, "we." There are more of what you would call "Holy Ones" than you could count. Of all races and species, of all creeds and colours, of all creation.'

'But all One.'

'And all One,' He agreed, gravely. 'It is ineffable, you know.'

And then we were giggling and it was the start of one of those laughter-fests when you can't stop. You simply can't; it just gets worse-better and worse-better until your jaw aches and you can barely control your bladder.

Once we'd stopped weeping with laughter, He took me on a journey to show me some of the miraculousness of it all ('hold my hand,' He said. 'You can only get where we're going if you hold my hand.' Oh, how I loved holding His hand…)

We went first to visit the heavens of the Rooted, Scented And Flowing Peoples, the spirits of nature on Earth. *Lord of the Rings* called some of them *Ents* and the Narnia stories told of *Dryads* and *Naiads* and there were thousands—no, millions—more even in the tiny patch of an entire world that we visited. It felt like deep-water diving in a world of swirling fish or, perhaps, like flying surrounded by birds. It was magical as this entire heaven swooped and dived and flowed and sang in a great and glorious murmuration of spirit. I could see some small places of intersection with what—for want of better words—I'll call indigenous or Pagan humanity and these, to me, were particularly beautiful. There was a dance of communion between these human spirits who loved and cherished nature which was breathtakingly enchanting.

'These are the spirits of humans who have chosen to live here,' He said. 'They were mostly hunter-gatherers and they knew the dance of life and death that Nature sustains—or did—on Earth. They knew that one day they would eat and another day, another aspect of life would eat. And that their bodies and souls gave back for everything they took. This is a symbiotic dance. Humanity for the most part has long forgotten it now. But it will be remembered again.'

'It will?'

'Oh yes. It all works out in the end. Remember that old teaching, "if it hasn't worked out yet, then you're not at the end of the story."? Humanity is still at the beginning of that story. You have a long way to go.'

'What about other species? On other planets? Or are we alone?'

'Alone?' He nearly fell over laughing at that one. 'You've never been alone! But you mean other sentience? Yes, of course. There are plenty and—again—you are only being shown your own story.'

'And do they all have their own Christ figures?' I asked, shyly. I'd long wanted to know the answer to this question.

'Yes. That's because the manifestation of Christ in a physical sense was never Plan B,' He said. 'It's always plan A. And there is always One alive in any world at any time; you just don't get to hear about 99.9999 per cent of them. Only very occasionally does one accidentally inspire a religion.'

'So… original sin…?'

He sighed. 'Dear old Augustine! And daft old Anselm… No, there's no such thing. Judaism never had any such concept, so how could anyone born into Judaism come to save you from it?'

'You know what would happen to you if you came back and said that!' I said.

'Yep.' He drew a finger across His throat. 'In retrospect, I caused a lot of harm.'

That did shock me.

'It wasn't you,' I said. I never thought I'd ever end up comforting *Him.* How utterly ridiculously surreal!

'Well, it was never intended,' He said. 'People seeking power picked it up and ran with it. And the clues are all there if you know where to look. You knew where to look, Beloved. Bel is short for 'beloved', you know.'

I thought my heart would explode for joy although I couldn't fully accept the compliment because I knew just how much I had looked in all the wrong places for so very long.

Next were the animal heavens which melded seamlessly with the environmental levels and there He showed me the lands of the extinct creatures from Earth. 'Nothing that has ever been loved is lost,' He said. 'And We love all creation. A species may be lost from Earth—and that indeed may be a sadness—but sometimes it has fulfilled its role and leaves voluntarily.

'And sometimes—just sometimes—you humans impede its transformation by insisting that the species is conserved! We often have a chuckle about that!'

'How can a creature fulfil its role?'

'By perfecting. That's the role of all creation; to become its perfect self. Once you have reached the pinnacle of your existence, it's time to move on to something else.'

'So what do they *do* here?' I asked watching a scene that could have been from *Jurassic Park*.

'That is their story,' He said, with a smile. 'You remember Aslan saying that you only get to hear your own story?'

'But you're telling me their story!'

'No, I'm telling you *about* their story.'

We spent some hours observing the higher fields of creation and wondrous it was. And in places (dodos, for example) joyfully ridiculous.

Then He took me to meet Metatron. As you do…

Again, not the *whole* Metatron but an aspect of Metatron. Metatron, by the way, is said to be part human and part angel, formerly Enoch from the Hebrew Testament.

'Enoch is there, yes,' He said. 'And Enoch is an aspect of Metatron. The essence of Metatron is that link between angel and human: the source of all guardian angels among other things—and yes, we are here to reclaim or rebuild your Hero.'

Mini-Metatron (for want of a better word) was golden-scarlet and a swirling of other colours I couldn't perceive with my limited human eyes. But I could see they were *there* even if I couldn't see what they were.

It didn't speak when He bowed to it but acknowledged the tribute.

Shouldn't It bow to you? I thought.

'Of course not. We do have hierarchies even here and in accordance to that, it is my turn to bow,' He said with a smile.

That was food for thought…

Together, we sat on another wooden park bench, this time eating an ice cream ('And why not?' He said, manifesting my favourite double raspberry Magnum from nowhere). We watched as Mini-Metatron wove energy into a cobweb, a feather, a being-ness. Then it gestured for me to come forward.

I hesitated.

'Go on,' He encouraged, taking the ice cream from me. 'It won't melt without you.' That wasn't exactly my primary concern!

'You're quite safe.' And He did laugh at me a little, for having the very thought that I might not be, but I didn't mind.

Cautiously, I stepped forward and Mini-Metatron began to weave the being-ness together with me. I've never thought about that spiritual idea of your 'aura' but now I could see mine, in swirls of colours and textures, all of which were being woven together with what I could now perceive to be an angel. I could sense an essence that was familiar—Hero!—but even so, this weave was subtly different. It was finer and stronger. I can't tell you how I knew that but it was so.

This was a glorious process. You know how sometimes you feel alone and lonely? (which is so very different from being contentedly alone). This was the healing of the very concept that anyone could ever be alone. We are all melded to our guardian angel and, through that angel, to all of the spirit world—to all creation.

Just as the joy seemed to become so great it was almost pain, the weaving ceased and the end result revealed. I was alight with my guardian; Hero—or more accurately *SuperHero*—was fully merged into my auric field; we were not two but not one either. We just were…

'A little bit of an upgrade,' He said, after I had, somewhat shakily, thanked Metatron who obviously wasn't used to that kind of thing and needed the idea explained to him.

My companion handed me back my ice cream which, miraculously, was complete again. 'The new model might need some running in.'

We both giggled. I was just about old enough to remember a time when new cars were thought to have to be 'run in' to work at full capacity.

Hero sparkled in reply and enclosed me in love which was more than reciprocated.

'Yes, she is the same angel and no, she is not,' He said in answer to my unspoken question.

'Ineffable?'

'Definitely!'

Metatron also wove me another Rus-el. Tall, red, armoured and still looking rather annoyingly like Russell Crowe in Gladiator. We bowed to each other but didn't speak.

Finally, we went to visit Marcus and Seraphim. I was slightly surprised, given the joy I had been experiencing throughout, how very special that was.

'Of course,' He said, smiling. 'These are personal; it matters.'

Seraphim was individuated and with Marcus when we arrived in that glorious, smelly, doggy realm. For the first time I saw other animals there, too, and understood that all relationships can be conserved and melded at every level. If a cat loved a dog, then why would they not continue to love in the heavens?

Seraphim raced over to us, squeaking with delight and simply couldn't work out who she wanted to jump up at more, Him or me. The three of us jumped up and down and raced round in circles, tongues hanging out and ears flapping. Okay… but that's how it felt.

At last, we all sat down in a kind of human-doggy heap and Marcus came over.

'Hello,' he said, prosaically. His smile though… his smile!

I stood up and put out my hand to shake his. Everyone laughed, including Seraphim.

Instead, Marcus put his own hand up as if to do a high five. I placed my palm against his and life-force flowed between us in a way that warmed my already-overflowing soul.

'I think I'm in love with you,' I blurted out. Jeez, Bel!

'Then we are both blessed,' he replied, raising my other hand to his lips. An odd response but a beautiful one, nonetheless.

'I have to apologise to you,' he said. 'I *was* there in your other universe but it was another of me and we had not fused consciousness when we last met so I did not remember. And it was my presence there which allowed the darkness to claim you.'

'You *did* have supper with me and tell me about your lives?'

'I did. And I ate your chocolate biscuits.'

'Oh…' that was marvellous to know. And yet, somewhat brain-frying too.

'There is some echo,' said Marcus. 'There is something yet to be realised. It is to do with this girl here.' He put his hand on the now-calm Seraphim's head. 'She still needs you and she will show you how.'

'Okay. You don't know why?'

'I don't. It has something to do with others that she loved who are not here yet. She, and our angels, will guide you to them when it is right. They believe you can help.'

'Of course I will—if I can.'

He smiled at me and we stood together, linked soul-to-soul for some moments while our guardians merged and talked. Even Marcus, who is part angel, had his own guardian—or at least a part of his essential self that could talk directly to Hero.

As we turned to Him, together, it felt strangely like a couple standing before a minister to marry.

Instead, He clapped us both on the back and laughed. 'And there's a conundrum!' He said. 'I'm going to enjoy watching you two work this one out!' It wasn't heartless; it was lovely because it *would* be enjoyment and, at this level—or at least one day, after my death—it *might* work out.

Somehow…

I woke up in my bed at home. I was fully dressed, including shoes, and had been beautifully tucked in by someone who obviously didn't know the first thing about duvets. It was still night time.

'What the…?' This was so much worse than waking up halfway through a wonderful dream. And far, far worse than missing the end of a totally engrossing movie.

Yes, for a few moments, I wished I were dead.

But at least, one day, I would be…

Memory streamed back as I lay there, recalibrating my brain.

Had I dreamt it *all*? Was I *totally* bonkers?

The sound of voices from downstairs reached me. Ah! Alessina and Robbie were here. Of course.

I shelved my disappointment and curiosity and got up. I could hear that Alessina was concerned at how long I had been absent. It was obviously far longer than just five minutes.

'I'm here!' I called from the top of the stairs. 'It's okay.'

Cautiously, I put both feet on the floor. I felt different; taller. I suppose that was the new-and-improved guardian angel aspect. Or maybe just the likely outcome of such an incredible experience.

The clock on the hall wall showed that I had been gone for about twenty Earth minutes, not long but quite long enough to evoke concern, if not outright panic, if you've said it would be five.

It was achingly hard to walk into an environment of worry when I had experienced such joy but it had to be done. And I was grateful for their concern and their love and their relief.

'Your hand?' said Alessina.

'My what? Oh! Yes, it's fine. Thanks.'

'Just "it's fine"?'

'Oh… so much has happened. But yes, it is. It is!' I beamed.

We had more tea. I'm one of the lucky ones who isn't affected by late-night tea or coffee. Robbie and Alessina, being much more discerning than me, had decaf and herbal.

I didn't tell them much; it was all too bright and too recent and too awe-inspiring. I found myself thinking over and over again. 'It's only and always love that sorts anything. And love to those who reject it is hell. So *that's* hell. But love even sorts that… well, eventually.'

There's only one spare bedroom in my home so Alessina shared my bed while Robbie slept in the spare room. She held me in her arms before we went to sleep and whispered, 'I can see that something amazing has happened to you. I'm so glad. Sleep well, darling girl.'

She was asleep in seconds. I lay awake for a while basking in that love too. Love is just so… well, lovely. Why do we resist it so much?

Chapter Eighteen

I DID FIND out later that the cosmic battle overhead dissolved the Archons (and I now suspect that it was a love-fuelled conflict on one side, at least, and that it only looked violent because of the reactions of the dark angels to that love). Maybe all of the Archons returned to fairies and angels and into love themselves? The evacuation of lost ones was completed—and all of their pets as well—and I found out that Jon, Callista and Sam hadn't been worried about me because they were 'debriefed' on their own level and, to be brutally honest, I was slightly miffed that no one had been concerned (egos are funny things, aren't they?) But once I'd got over my mini-huff I wished that life could be as full of such clear communication down here.

Hero didn't make herself known that morning. I had to trust she was there and in the meantime I had some exorcism work to do. That was a tad scary. But then she was only obviously present when I needed her so there was nothing to worry about yet.

This was, of course, if we could actually find the twins…

Robbie and Alessina were bright and bouncy at breakfast; I felt tired and slightly depressed. Possibly a reaction, possibly anticipation of the week ahead. Whatever it was, I felt quite relieved when Mrs Tiggy phoned to say that the twins had gone AWOL.

'As in this morning or overnight?' I asked her when she telephoned.

'This morning. Their Mum dropped them off here and they went outside to play. I told them we were going over to yours and they just vanished.'

I bet they did, I thought.

Lucie turned up though… and Will, so it was still going to be a busy morning. Lucie heralded her advent with a text asking 'R U Okehampton? Just about to Pope in. Will fond you coop of Gym of the Cheerleaders.' As far as I could ascertain, autocorrect and locational services had transformed 'OK' to the name of our local market town and systematically changed her religion. The last bit was beyond me.

Will's arrival was the moment new-and-improved Hero came into her own. No running in required!

I went to answer the doorbell, expecting my assistant-cum-takeover-cleric and my heart sank when I saw it was Will; I still didn't know how to relate to him after the parallel universe situation. But Hero did. Oh thank God, I could feel her!

She filled the space before me and questioned Will's guardian. I could sense the communication quite clearly and Will himself hesitated on the doorstep as he felt it subconsciously too. Neither of us said a word until the angels had circled and then embraced each other.

Safe, said Hero in my head and the tension simply dissolved.

'Hello Will,' I said. 'This is a surprise. Come in.'

'I brought you something,' he said, with a bashful smile, handing me a CD by Tchaikovsky. 'It has that *Hymn of the Cherubim* that you love on it.'

'Oh, how kind.'

It *was* kind but it was also slightly cloying. When would this man realise that I simply wasn't interested? I'd already bought an mp3 of that exquisite music but obviously it wouldn't be remotely polite to tell him so. Fortunately, I realised that this must be the 'Gym of the Cheerleaders' that Lucie was referring to and my amusement did, at least, look like genuine gratitude.

You are still expecting vicars to be nice, aren't you? We do our best but the ends of our tethers wind a little closer every year.

Lucie's pink VW drew up outside as we were still standing there and we all went in together, so there was quite a crowd of us in the kitchen when the ceiling fell in.

Those *sodding* kids! They had snuck into the house somehow and overflowed the basin in the bathroom so the floor flooded, dripped pathetically for a couple of moments, just enough to get us all looking up in surprise, before dropping a pile of water and wet plaster on our heads.

We caught them because they were too eager to see the fun of the destruction they had brought. Or, more accurately, Will and Robbie caught them. Will went up in my estimation immediately by bringing Oliver downstairs by holding his ear between finger and thumb. I had never seen that well-remembered practice from old children's books actually carried out but it was obviously highly effective. Robbie carried Iris down in both arms and suffered a bloody nose for it as she hit out at him indiscriminately.

'Id's odkay,' Robbie said as he put her down in the remnants of the kitchen and mopped his substantial conk with a linen handkerchief. 'I'b sure id's dot broken.'

Alessina moved in front of Iris as she tried to run away and fixed her with an eagle eye.

'He hit me!' alleged Iris, almost certainly mendaciously but, with plaster in my hair, my own bloody nose, a possible black eye and a ruined kitchen, I wasn't going to enquire too closely. And yes, I have done my safeguarding courses lately *and* I do know that demonic possession isn't mentioned in any of them.

'Let me *go!*' yelled Oliver. 'I'm reporting you!' Will had set him down on a very dusty-damp chair and was still holding his ear in a way that meant that if Oliver didn't move, he wouldn't get hurt.

Iris stamped on Alessina's foot and found herself being lifted and held upside down by a very powerful witch. Alessina refrained from going full Librarian and banging Iris's head on the floor (which probably *would* have been a safeguarding issue, demons or no demons) but held her firmly around the waist, pinning her arms while she screamed and tried to kick out with legs tucked very firmly into Alessina's chest.

I tottered to my study to collect the holy water and a crucifix and, once there, paused for a moment to pull myself together. It was so very tempting to allow rage to flow over but that could only bring more danger. It was more important to stop the rot now before it could spread.

We did the exorcism, Robbie and I, while Lucie held onto Will, who was round-eyed with a combination of horror and fear and quite likely to interfere. How could he possibly know what was going on?

The demons resisted, of course, but the guardians of the children helped and, when it was done, both Oliver and Iris themselves were glad; you could see them being restored, relieved and re-set into your average naughty kids instead of being driven by that extra level of viciousness that made all the difference. 'It felt like I was being bitten,' said Oliver once he was fully Oliver again. We didn't explain exactly what had happened; luckily modern New Age terminology like 'bad energy fields' are relatively acceptable now and we could just tell them they had picked up some very bad vibes.

Once everyone was themselves again, we all decamped to the living room and had a glass of the remaining elderflower cordial that I had made the previous year from glorious, frothing blossom that cascaded through most of the local hedges in early summer. I didn't fancy it for some reason so only had a sip or two. The children sat silently on the sofa, looking exhausted. Iris could barely hold her glass so Alessina held it for her, radiating comfort and kindness. Will and Lucie held hands (a very good sign!) and, bless her, Lucie explained to him, quietly. The two of them were grey with plaster and still damp (as were we all) but unhurt. I was *so* grateful that in *this* universe there had been no Will opening my door first thing to a shocked and hurt Lucie.

'It was a special blessing for clearing destructive energies that Amabel and Robbie were taught to do by our previous bishop,' she said, accurately and with perfect, partial truth. 'The children needed it and it's all over now. You can see they both look better.' I could have kissed her. Lucie hadn't known beforehand that the children were possessed but although she's ditsy, she certainly isn't dim. Moreover, she had her own experience to draw on.

I managed to call Mrs Tiggy without bleeding over the telephone and she arrived in haste, giving short shrift to two slightly defiantly repentant grandchildren who didn't really know what on Earth was going on but perfectly understood that what they planned as a prank had led to rather serious consequences.

She gathered the children up like a fierce mother hen and drove them home where, I suspect, they would never hear the end of it (good!) and we debriefed ourselves, washed, applied bandages, salves and sticking plaster and did what we could to clear up the kitchen.

'This is going to take some sorting,' said Will. 'Where do you start? Plumber? Builder? And will your insurance pay?'

'Mrs Tiggy's daughter should pay,' said Robbie who was rubbing the top of his chest as if experiencing heartburn.

I left them to it, discussing how to sort out the kitchen and whether anyone knew someone handy who could do it or whether they should get onto the local Facebook group. Obviously it was my business but I needed some 'me' time. Even having people staying for one night was tiring enough for a singleton like me, let alone the events of the day before and the extraordinary night in the heavens. I think I could be forgiven for needing some space.

Trying to disconnect my brain, I wandered over to St. Raphael's through the churchyard, one hand trailing, idly, over the lichen on the ancient tombstones of the Wonnacotts and the Pearsons of this parish. The snowdrops had passed while I was in hospital but celandines peeped out of the grass at the foot of the stones, awaiting the moment when they would suddenly strengthen and leap up in the shared joy of the new year's progress into spring. Halfway along the path, I saw a yew aril on the ground and remembered Alessina's jam. Idly, my brain considered other ways you could poison people with foraged foods. Mushrooms of course, Lords and Ladies, Nightshade, Giant Hogweed, Hemlock… the list went on. Giant Hemlock and Hogweed, of course, look somewhat similar to Elderflower—*shit!* Burning in the digestive tract was one of the symptoms of Hemlock poisoning…

I was crashing in through the French windows of the Old Rectory before my lungs had time to protest at the unfamiliar speed and enthusiasm of my legs.

'Robbie! Are you okay? Is everyone okay?' I spluttered.

Alessina, Will, Robbie and Lucie all had their backs to the window. They turned their heads to look at me. 'Oh! You're okay; you're okay; thank God,' I said. 'I thought…'

Then I saw at whom they had been looking when I raced in. Yes, the good old bishop had sent the requisite Approved Mental

Health Professional to visit the doolally vicar who was currently ranting like a lunatic and looked as though a ceiling had fallen on her head.

The AMHP was a determined-looking woman with a short cap of straight grey hair. She introduced herself as Sarah Oldman, social worker, shook my hand with that familiar Funeral Director caring/patronising two-handed grip, smiled at me kindly, looked me over from top to bottom without letting go of my hand and asked if it might be convenient to have a word with me in private, alongside my nearest relative, of course.

She spoke slowly and carefully in case I was unable to understand normal speech and her smile was so deeply caring that I nearly turned into a puddle of saccharine.

Still, at least no one had been poisoned with Hemlock.

Yet.

I don't have a 'nearest relative' but Alessina volunteered and, given that the hospital in Exeter had her down as 'wife,' she would certainly do.

'Oh good,' said Ms Oldman. 'We can begin now.'

So we did. But even with my dearest friend there, it wasn't going to go well, was it? Yes, I did have the excuse of the kitchen ceiling genuinely falling on me and that might give anyone the heebie-jeebies but it was really quite a challenge answering Ms Oldman's questions without sounding totally bonkers. And I could only admit that I *had* hit my bishop so, as she said, either I needed psychiatric help or I would have to face charges.

'Of course, his Grace doesn't want to go down that road,' she said. 'It would bring the Church into even more disrepute. I think it's important for you to have a proper psychiatric assessment so I have organised one for you on Monday in Exeter. They'll be able to tell if you need to be sectioned or not.'

'*Sectioned*?' said Alessina.

'Worst case scenario,' said Ms Oldman briskly. 'But Reverend Ransom currently cannot clarify the reasons for her actions and these have become steadily more erratic.'

'Is saving the bishop's life from an attacker, erratic?' asked Alessina, quietly.

'His Grace says the brick went nowhere near him,' said Ms Oldman. 'And yet, Reverend Ransom leapt on him.'

'Not true,' I said. But, in all fairness, my recollection of the event was not totally clear. I was battling an undercurrent of panic. It was *entirely* possible, with all that had been going on, that I wasn't actually firing on all cylinders (which would be a polite way of looking at it).

'I have a suggestion to make,' said my friend, again quietly and with dignity. 'Bel is long overdue for a holiday. We all know that she has had a serious head injury some time ago and a lesser one recently. I concur that she is not fully herself but I believe that much of this is exhaustion. She is diligent in taking care of her congregation and such devotion to duty can lead to overwork. What say you to her taking a couple more weeks of rest—with her friends taking care of her—and then having that assessment? It wouldn't be as effective an evaluation if the subject is clearly exhausted.'

Hold, said Hero as I prepared to jump in. I shut up and tried to look intelligent, engaged and suitably submissive which probably made me look like a bemused kitten who's just taken a mouthful of superglue.

Alessina does transmit power and Ms Oldman was aware of it. Social workers are—in my experience—of two kinds, the ones who work with intuition and the ones who do it by the book. The intuitive ones have a harder time of it because they can't necessarily explain what it was that alerted them to a possible problem. But, also, they are the ones who are prepared to take a chance when their heart or gut tells them to.

I think we can all guess which one Ms Oldman was going to turn out to be. Not that I'm suggesting she was a part of the Dark Side but even Obi Wan Kenobi copped it in the end, didn't he?

'Of course, such an innovative idea can be considered at the assessment on Monday,' she said and I would swear that doves outside must have been listening in for a masterclass on how to coo.

It was at that point that the cars started turning up for the wedding.

At least it wasn't my marriage; it was Lucie's, as I was already taking a backseat so, for once, it wasn't me who had to thunder over to the church going 'shit, shit, shit, *shit!*' Not that Lucie would ever thunder and it would be 'Oh goodness gracious!' as she never gives voice to anything remotely offensive. But she obviously had forgotten and I saw her running across the churchyard with her mouth open in a horrified 'O.' It did, at least, give me the chance to send Ms Oldman on her way as I could justifiably insist that I had to go and assist my assistant who didn't need any assistance at all.

Oh what a day we were having…

Chapter Nineteen

'It's Catch 22, isn't it?' said Jon, that evening. 'You submit to a mental health hearing and either have to lie your head off or tell the truth and face being sectioned. They won't want to take you to court because of the scandal.'

'Either way, I'm stuffed,' I said. 'I suspect this could be the end of the road for my being a vicar.'

That hurt. Whether or not I'm a heretic, and a grumpy one at that, I do love my work and what else could I do? Let's face it, we all need to pay the bills.

'Going to court might be the third way. You never know. Maybe it's worth a try?'

'All right,' said Jon. 'We need to consider what's *really* happening here. We believe the bishop is possessed and by a not-very-smart demon, because a smart one would never hurt you or provoke you if there was a potential witness. So is this a plot to get you removed from your earthly work? And, if so, why? You can continue working with me for as long as you want to whatever you do for a living. Unless…' he paused.

'Unless?'

'Well, if you are assessed as mentally ill then you'll be put on whatever the appropriate drugs are for your alleged condition and *then* you might not be able to travel with me.'

'And those drugs might be chosen with exactly that intent?'

'Shockingly possible.'

'Shit.'

'Shit indeed. Maybe the demon isn't that dumb after all.'

'There's still Gerry. If he was called as a witness, he'd have to say what he had seen. But who would believe that the bishop was hitting me first? Gerry could lose his job, too.'

'And if you go to court and lose, you'll be defrocked.'

'If I go to court and win…?'

'I'd say that's not really a win. Not one that counts. It would preclude your ever working in this area again. No one sensible would think that you and the bishop could work together no matter how forgiving you might be seen to be in public. And if you don't get the demon out of him, there would be more weird stuff to come. So, at the very best, you'd have to move to a new parish—and find one that would take you. I suspect that after *any* court case the Anglican Church would prefer that even an acquitted defendant quietly dissolved into the ether and was never seen again.'

'I'm screwed then,' I said, glumly, as the blue Panda emerged over Kyiv. We had other Ukrainian cities to help out with apart from Mariupol and just because a figurative Sword of Damocles was hanging over my head was no excuse not to focus on the Work.

Speaking of Swords of Damocles, there were bound to be Archons here, too. I could perceive two of them under the clouds but, for some reason, they retreated as we drove down.

'They're scared of you,' said Jon, smiling.

'What?'

'You're our secret weapon now. You dissolved an Archon with love. Word of terrorist activities like that gets out fast.'

'Terrorist?!'

'That's what you're like to them. Terrifying.'

'I'm not sure I could do that again.' Of course I could if He were there but what if He weren't?

'Don't worry. We've got a space while they regroup. They *will* regroup but we can, hopefully, get all the souls out before they do.'

There might not have been a heavenly battle overhead but, even so, we still had our work cut out in Kyiv. Callista and Sam humoured me as I insisted on trying to find a yew tree first, just in case, but when we asked where the nearest *tysove derevo* might be, none of the Earthbound had heard of one. Turns out yew trees are pretty rare in Eastern Europe.

This night we worked with other living Earth humans and

their celestial counterparts; the first time I had come across others like me. We didn't speak; there seemed to be some pre-agreed principle that getting to know each other on this side would be too complicated in lives that were essentially wrapped in secrecy. But we did acknowledge each other and it was *so* good to know that there was a team of us. And that we were of all different faiths, too; I saw two women in hijabs, a couple of Jewish men in yarmulkes, three women in saris and four men in throbes. There was also a vicar in a dog collar; a man, about fifty perhaps, with a strong face and Roman nose. He couldn't know I was a vicar too but we waved. As you do.

'Were these others in Mariupol too?' I asked Sam.

'Yes.' he answered. 'You'd done the clearing so they could get in.'

'You and I were first in?'

'Yes. The Archons had made it impossible but we thought, given your knowledge of the Universal Christ Consciousness, you might just have a shot.'

'And if I'd failed?'

'Well, that's someone else's story, isn't it? You didn't fail. You did brilliantly.'

I blushed. It's nice when someone tells you that you are brilliant. But I had more questions.

'Remind me again why you need us at all,' I said.

'Your energy is denser than ours. The etheric dead can often only see us through you. You're recognisable.'

'Aren't you?'

'No, it's all a matter of frequency.'

'So I'm dense,' I said, just to push the point.

'Indeed you are,' said Sam, gravely, patting me on the back.

'So what about Jon and Callista? They're both dead.'

'Hmmm. Well, Jon's association with you lowers his vibration…'

'Really?'

'Afraid so!' Sam grinned. 'You make your brother denser so he can—albeit briefly—do the same job as you.'

'Oh.' I wasn't sure what to make of the idea that I made Jon denser.

'Glad your hand is better,' said Sam, changing the subject with dexterity, tact and diplomacy.

'Me too.' A human and a ghost grinned at each other and got on with their job.

That night we found dozens of people, many of them unaware that they were dead. Without the Archons—were they *all* afraid of that Presence of Love who had walked into one with me?—it was a far simpler matter to guide the lost ones through. Some needed the call of the silvery sphere that represented their soul; others dissolved into the ether of their own accord.

'It depends on what they believe about death and what their level of consciousness was while they lived,' said Sam. 'Some are Earthbound; some are just shocked out of the realisation that they can go through.'

'But we never actually tell them that they are dead.'

'No, we don't. It's another vibrational thing; difficult to explain.'

'I expect it's ineffable,' I said, glumly.

'That'd work!' Sam grinned. 'Seriously, though, have you lost sight of the guardians?'

I had. But now he had alerted me, my spirit sight woke up and I started to see lights around the people we approached. Their angels were still with them, though often weakened and pale. However, strengthened by our own guardians, they could call their people to recognition that there was somewhere they needed to go. Some of the humans intuitively knew this was their angel; some believed it was a friend and some were just grateful there was some kind of signpost to the way out.

But much more interesting was the Cat Wrangler. Marcus and his thousands of also-Marcus acolytes had already fetched all the dogs in Kyiv so the cats could come out of hiding. Their angel-human was a far more complex affair, prowling around the ruined city presenting as anything between ten and ninety-five per cent cat according to the relationship each creature had experienced with humanity. I watched her in fascination as she and her different aspects courted, lured, loved and snarled at the lost felines. She seemed to me to be more like a panther than a cat, the Queen Of All Cats if you like, and the spirits responded to her almost as though they had returned to dependent kittenhood. Mind you, if you told them that on the other side they'd have fixed you with a glare, stalked away in disgusted denial and ignored you for a week.

We saw the Turtle Wrangler and the Caged Bird Wrangler. Neither had much they needed to do but it was still essential for creatures who had never lived with their own kind to have some kind of human-ish guide—'ish' being the appropriate terminology. The seven pet turtles raised in the city swam through to the other dimension and all the Caged Bird Wrangler had to do was reinstate the cage and open the door so the birds could fly. And oh, did they fly! Up and up and up with cries of joy.

I often found myself weeping with both sadness and joy as the dance of restitution and repair continued. We humans have tamed so much, rightly or wrongly, and it was powerful knowing that the heavens—and the humans—could and would adapt to ensure that very little was lost. I wish I could say 'nothing was lost' but, occasionally, we came across a soul who wasn't interested in moving on and preferred to live like a homeless person in the shadows. If that person had a pet, their pet generally remained too.

'What do we do now?' I asked Sam as we were spat at by a former human and growled at by his dog.

'Nothing,' he said. 'Even at this level there is free will. But you'll see in a few minutes that when the clearing is finished, the city will change and those who still want to remain will become a part of the shadowlands—living in a kind of copy of where they are now—you know, the place where we usually go to retrieve folk. There we can monitor them and bring their souls to try and guide them through. There are always folk visiting those lands and they have ways of telling if and when people change their minds.'

'But his dog...?'

'... Would rather be with him,' said Sam, firmly, moving me on.

It was a long night but just before dawn we had cleared all that was willing to clear and there was a sense of closure. Without anyone saying anything specific, our angels gathered together the helper souls in kind of vortex on the edge of the city. It felt as though all the angels were holding hands—an extraordinary and deep sense of connection filled me and I could see from the others' faces that they felt the same.

Then the magic began.

Our angels began to sing, softly and low at first and rising into one united voice that called to and revealed the angels of the trees, of the river, of the underground waters, of the flowers and the churches and of the homes and the shops—'*Everything* has an angel,' whispered Sam in my ear—and their voices rose in patterned droplets of light above the ruined city, adding harmony, timbre and depth to this strange spiralling clarion call.

The music swelled; it did not get louder, it expanded. It grew like a foetus while thrumming in my body like the bass at a rock concert and delighting my heart with its strange beauty. At its zenith, it shattered into millions of shards of seeming-starlight and the spirit of the city itself reformed into elegant buildings, streets and parks, shimmering and incandescent.

'The heavenly Jerusalem!' I said, awed.

'The heavenly Kyiv,' said Sam. 'But it will do.'

It would more than do.

'Nothing that has ever been loved is ever lost,' said Jon, appearing behind me. 'It can take its time, of course but, in the end, we all come home.'

'Even the ones who don't want to?'

'Even the ones who don't want to. Eventually, even the most prodigal children decide to go home.'

'Oh I hope you're right.'

'Ineffably,' said Jon with a chuckle.

That night, I dreamt of the other vicar I had seen in Kyiv. He and his astral companion—an albino female soul—were digging under a building. I couldn't help them as I was observing rather than present but I could feel my hands itching to join in as they scrabbled through rubble.

Eventually they found a child, a little boy about six years old curled up with a white German Shepherd bitch. The boy lifted his arms up to my vicar friend to be lifted out but the dog growled when the man tried to reach her. She sat up and I could see she was a lactating bitch with three tiny white puppies and my heart broke for her. Even in protecting her own brood, she had tried also to provide shelter for the child of her people.

'What do we do?' the man asked his beautiful, eerie companion. She was more like an elf from *The Lord of the Rings* than a human and although I'm calling her 'she' it was only because of long, silvery hair. The being itself appeared genderless; if I hadn't been so emotionally involved with the dog I would have stared at her in wonder. She stood, tall and straight, somehow glowing, holding the child in her arms and an essence of healing within her was visibly flowing into him.

'I do not know,' she said.

'Call Marcus!' I said out loud but how could they hear me?

'I can't leave her,' said the man and I loved him for that.

'I must take the boy,' said the woman. 'We must leave now.'

'No, I'll stay. Can you find out what to do and come back?' said the man.

'You wish to stay?'

'No, but I *must* stay.'

'Very well.' She turned away. I wasn't sure whether she was actually human. I don't think Jon would ever have agreed to leave me behind like that.

In the dream, the elf vanished and the man sat down beside the dog and spoke gently to her. He was speaking English and she was a Ukrainian dog so he was on somewhat of a hiding to nothing but his voice was gentle and reassuring and he remained still so as not to frighten her more. She looked at him long and hard and then, to both his and my surprise, she leant into him and sighed. He began to cry. He reached out one shaking hand to her and she licked it.

'Oh Marcus, Marcus, *Marcus!*' I cried in the dream but who could hear me?

Seraphim. That's who.

She was there, from nowhere, scrabbling down through the rubble to stand beside the man with her ears cocked forwards, communicating with the white German Shepherd who looked up and spoke back. Seraphim did the hound equivalent of an acknowledgment, gazed at me (truly!) and then vanished.

'No!' I cried.

But she had gone to fetch Marcus. Bless that hound! Together now, they were clambering down into the half-buried room and Marcus was calling gently to the young mother in dog language. She could hear and see him and her ears flickered back and forwards in affectionate greeting. She trusted him so much she showed him her puppies. They were only a few weeks old. Marcus spoke with her again and I could tell that she agreed that he could pick the puppies up and take them with him. But then, strangely, she indicated what she would not go with him herself. Sadly, she licked the little squirming bodies in his arms as if kissing them goodbye and then she went to stand beside the man.

Marcus talked to her gently and then turned to the man.

'She wishes to stay with you to help other dogs come through,' he said. 'She will live as a ghost in your home if you permit it.'

'But how could she be happy doing that? These are her puppies!' said the man. I noted that he didn't say 'no.'

'Do you know the loving heart of a dog?' said Marcus.

'I do,' said the man. 'I once had a lovely girl just like her, when I was young. She was called Margot.'

'This *is* Margot,' said Marcus. 'She is now remembering you. She wishes to stay with you as her latest family had many dogs to be reunited with and they will not miss her particularly.'

Then the man truly wept. And Margot, remembering him fully, moved closer to him and began to lick his hands.

I woke with tears in my own eyes. And the feeling that I was not alone. Something was curled up asleep in the small of my back. Seraphim had come home.

Chapter Twenty

THE NEXT DAY was Sunday; a day of respite before the gathering storm. Robbie and I watched the rank and file gathering at St. Raphael's with Lucie greeting them at the church door. She looked ethereally beautiful in her white alb.

'She has a true vocation and an almost disturbing innocence,' said Robbie, slightly wistfully.

'And so do you,' I replied, touching his arm. Robbie was always so insecure; rarely felt loved at any time in his life and had probably first turned to God out of sheer loneliness. It was easy to see the inner beauty in Lucie but Robbie had ample, too; he just didn't believe it. Occasionally, when he was my assistant, he had told me stories of being bullied at school, of distant parents wrapped up in their own problems and of boarding-school sexual abuse. He didn't project blame but, almost worse, seemed not to have expected that he deserved anything better. The spirit world is terribly efficient in mirroring our beliefs about us back to us.

'You should get a dog,' I said, apropos of nothing. I suppose it was my way of saying 'I wish you love.'

It was a foolish remark because we then had to discuss the possibilities of Robbie having a dog, what kind of dog, whether he actually liked dogs or whether a cat would be better and what he would do with said pet if he had to go away and what would happen if any dog bit a parishioner (I did say Robbie was a worrier, didn't I?)

'A mixed-breed, rescue dog,' suggested Alessina, briskly, when she turned up around lunchtime to check that all was well. 'That will give you enough angst as you deal with whatever issues it arrives with and a ton of unconditional love as you learn to trust each other.'

We were all sitting in the kitchen, the heart of my home. I said nothing, watching in fascination as Robbie's hand moved to stroke Seraphim without realising it. She was very nearly visible to me now, a certain hound-shaped shimmer in space, and Robbie was sensing her unconsciously. Alessina saw too and grinned at me.

'Unless you want a rehomed foxhound or beagle, of course,' she said. 'Hunts are always looking for people to adopt hounds which don't care to drag hunt.'

'Can you train a dog to run beside your bicycle?' said Robbie, that archetypical vicar, who toured as much as he could of his parish on a battered sit-up-and-beg cycle.

'Yes,' said Alessina. 'And most parish visits go better with a dog. It gives you something to talk about.'

With Robbie, that was a very good point. Bless him, he had the humility to see the truth in that.

Lucie joined us for a lunch of home-made roasted pepper and garlic soup with sourdough from the village shop and the two of them managed to divert her away from fussing over me. Finally, Lucie, Robbie and Alessina all headed home and I was left in peace with my ghost hound.

We went for a walk. I love St. Raphael's and all the other churches in the parish (we are totally blessed in the rural south west with the most beautiful Norman buildings) but Dartmoor is my heart's church; the place where I can wander and listen to both to God and to Mother Nature.

On the other side of St. Raphael's, through an old wicket gate, is an artist's palette of dark greens, browns and greys. The ever-cleansing moorland wind caressed me as I stomped along the sheep-made paths. It was a little too cold for comfort but the briskness helped to blow away the cobwebs of my mind. I was joyfully aware of my ghost hound racing ahead and around me as I started climbing up over the first hill to the brim of a small valley, currently encrusted with shockingly-bright yellow gorse flowers. Here, the wind-bent grey willows and the moor behind them revealed themselves in all their beauty. No matter what is going on in my life, every single time that view unfolds itself my mouth curves up into a smile as broad as Julia Roberts's.

This day, the sky was cold turquoise blue, clustered with cirrus clouds, and the sun shone nearly white with a pale golden aureole. Shaggy bay Dartmoor ponies foraged between the patches of stumpy bronze bracken and I wished I could offer them more sustenance but it is a dangerous game to feed wild ponies as you can easily harm them. It was interesting to note that Seraphim spooked them when she ran, tongue hanging out, parallel to where they grazed. I wondered, idly, if she would, perhaps, find a ghost fox and how on Earth that would pan out!

When I climb our local hills I love to look out for the still, clear pools of water that nestle in peated hollows between the gorse bushes. They always remind me of the world between the worlds depicted in the *Magician's Nephew* and I shake my head in wonder that I have actually been there.

It's always wise to get back home before the early winter dusk as it is so easy to get lost on the moorland. But some nights, when the weather is clear, I venture out just a little way to bask in the starlight away from even the miniscule village light pollution. The stars viewed from here are so beautiful they sing through my heart and soul.

Here, I can stand or sit or lie and watch the sky unfold before me as my eyes adjust to the night. The whole Universe comes and wraps itself into my heart so I am a part of the cosmic dust—completely caught up in the organic presence of it.

With a slight shock, I realised that I had not been out wondering at this Earthly night for more than a year—since I began travelling with Jon. I made a mental note to take more nights off so that I could reclaim the magic of my own, living world, rather than spending *all* my nights with the dead.

And then I chuckled because I do get to travel *through* those stars most nights. It's just another form of magic.

This day, Seraphim and I stayed out until the gloaming sank its softness into the land. I let my mind wander as it wished for a while and then settled it, as I sat beneath one of those windswept willows, to connect, listen and learn.

By the time ghost hound and I were on our way home I knew what I had to do.

*

I was polite enough to send a message to Ms. Oldman to tell her that I was not going to show up to the Monday psychiatric assessment and that I fully understood that this would mean that the bishop might wish to press charges against me. Message sent, I then turned off my laptop and telephone, disconnected the answerphone on the landline, absorbed myself in Catherine Fox's wonderful *Lindchester Chronicles* and, when Jon showed up, told him I wanted the night off.

'Yes of course,' he said.

'You what?!' he said when I told him my plans.

But I was adamant. You can't say (even to your dead brother) 'It's what God wants me to do,' but I truly believed it was. It was certainly *a* third way, if not *the* third way.

When he left I took a torch, and a ghost hound, out onto Dartmoor to lie on the cold ground and gaze at the stars.

There were no messages on Monday or on Tuesday. I was half expecting to be picked up and taken to the police station in Okehampton to be charged officially with racially-motivated common assault, with the likely outcome of a fine or a six-month prison sentence. It was unlikely that I would be denied bail although I might be forbidden to go anywhere near the bishop which would put any passing exorcism work out of the window but was only to be expected.

But nothing happened. Slightly perplexed, I wondered if wiser counsel had prevailed and that I might just (just!) face a Church Disciplinary Procedure. That was the normal way of dealing with recalcitrant priests but nothing was really normal here.

In the meantime, each night I went back to the Ukraine with Jon, Sam and Callista. City after city, we walked through in the debris of war working with the other souls in clearing, blessing and healing. Seraphim came with us and, just as Alessina had said to Robbie, the presence of a dog often helped, particularly with children.

Marcus and the other 'pet angels' were sometimes there and sometimes not. The other humans were around, too, and I could now perceive that some of them had animals as well—a little like the daemons in Philip Pulman's *His Dark Materials* although these were all former pets rather than aspects of the soul. I saw the grey-haired man with the dog collar so many times that we started to acknowledge each other's presence with a wave in passing. His ghost dog, Margot, was there too which perplexed me because I had only dreamt that encounter.

'*Only* dreamt?' said Jon, when I asked him about it. 'I suspect it was a lucid dream and those are always on a different level. You dreamt it because you couldn't actually be there at that time but you needed to know for some reason. It will unfold in its own good time.'

'But it's getting to the stage with parallel realities and dreams that I don't know what's real anymore!'

'No, it's getting to the stage where you are seeing more options and can choose which path you take. You told me that this man's guide seemed to be more Lord of the Rings elfin than human?'

'Yes, silvery and gender-fluid.

'And how do you see that guide now, here?'

'As a woman with fair hair.'

'Okay, well you saw a higher truth in your dream. We souls don't have a gender. We present to you as a gender—and as we used to look in our last incarnation, mostly—though we can choose so as not to freak you out.'

'Becoming denser so we can perceive you.'

'Exactly. We don't *function* as male or female but we do accept the *role* of being male of female.'

A long-lost memory surfaced, making me laugh.

'I used to think I didn't want to go to heaven because it didn't have sex. I guess if you have no gender to identify with, there's something better?'

'*Much* better,' said Jon with a big grin. 'Much, *much* better.'

'But beyond my pay grade.'

'Definitely!.'

'So all the fuss and bother about gender on Earth is, in the higher worlds, irrelevant?'

'It's not irrelevant on Earth but it is attaining too high an importance. People are over-identifying with the roles of the sexes; that's one of the things that leads to the cosmetic surgery industry—the role of youth is also desired because of the roles of gender. The *function* of gender is reproduction, nurturing and sexual. The *role* of gender is whatever society says it is.'

'Okay, so if you no longer have a sex, why does Sam work with me and you work with Callista?'

'To get the balance right at the human level,' said Jon. 'It's part of what Gurdjieff was teaching about the density of worlds.'

'You know I can't handle Gurdjieff!'

'Then try Cynthia Bourgeault. She's a mystic and she interprets this well in her *Eye of the Heart.*'

'Was that published when you were alive?'

'No, but we all gave a big cheer when she wrote it. She wrote it from the level your dream showed you.'

'I'm still pretty dense then.'

'You're still *very* dense, Bel,' said Jon, and quoted the professor from C. S, Lewis's *The Lion, The Witch and the Wardrobe*: 'What *do* they teach them in these schools?'

When nothing had arrived from the Bishop's Palace or the police station by Wednesday lunchtime, I sent a polite email around the entire diocese saying that, as I was still on recovery leave from the brick-throwing incident, I was going on holiday for a fortnight and would be uncontactable by any device whatsoever.

What I needed was a holiday. Ah, winter sunshine on the beach, you may think. Maybe that missed trip to Israel? No, I went to Brussels.

It's called trusting God or, in layman's terms, being a bloody idiot. I just knew from my contemplation on the moor that this was the right thing to do. At least this time I could book a room in advance and use my debit cards. Also, I could take my ghost dog. She seemed to be remarkably enthusiastic about it. So much so that I remembered that she still needed something from me. Maybe it was in Brussels?

I travelled without fear and enjoyed the experience of the train from Okehampton to Exeter, another to Waterloo, the tube to Kings Cross and a short walk to St. Pancras where the Eurostar took me under the sea to Brussels.

Brussels is still surprisingly lovely and yes, I did have a gaufre on the way to my 'boutique' hotel. I was planning a kind of walking exorcism of the previous experience and, once that was done, simply to have a break. I could go on to Lille if I wanted to, or to Bruges. Or anywhere.

I did plan to say hello to St. Michael and St. Gudula at the Cathedral. Michael, being an archangel, should have his representative angel in the sanctuary—and this time I might see it—and although St. Gudula shouldn't be hanging around, being human and long dead and all that, I could still buy a lamp in her honour. However, having done some research on her, I wasn't all that sure she was really my kind of saint. You can have a tad too much saintliness in a family. To lose one child to saintliness is fortunate, to lose five seems excessive. Worse (or better, depending on your point of view), both Gudula's mother and grandfather were saints as well as her sisters and brothers. Maybe there was a BOGOF on holiness in the seventh century.

The mother of this slightly worrying clusterfaith went into a convent after having her children which, let's face it, would be seen nowadays as abandonment, not holiness, especially as her children were raised in other monastic houses so she didn't even have to see them. In the seventh century, however, they didn't have social media to troll her to her senses. Saint Amalberga was married to Count Witger, Duke of Lorraine, who also hi-tailed it off to a monastery himself just after Gudula was born so I guess Amalberga didn't have a lot of choice. It is, of course, possible that she couldn't stand her five holy children and did a kind of runner herself and I guess none of the kids were offered a wide range of career options. I can imagine hanging out with that particular family would have been an absolute riot.

Count Witger, apparently, did not become a saint which was, frankly, just carelessness. I like to think that he might have become one of those rather jolly monks who kept bees and maybe even a mistress, drank a lot of mead and thanked God every day that he was ensconced in a place where humility was valued more than saintliness.

Absolutely nothing is known of *why* any of the above seven

holy people were considered saintly apart from Gudula's habit of getting up before dawn to pray and so deeply annoying the devil when she did it that he tried to blow out her lantern. What he was doing hanging out around her place before dawn is anybody's guess but then, demons seem to hang around me too so we actually do have something in common.

But that bright, frosty Bruxellian day appeared devoid of demons and the Cathedral was calm and lovely. The angel in the sanctuary acknowledged my prayer for its blessing but this time it unfurled six salmon-pink and gold wings that were almost certainly an optical illusion for my benefit and a fabulously beautiful one indicating that the angel truly was 'Of Michael' and not just your common or garden one. I thanked him, hand on heart, and he bowed to me.

Priestess, I heard.

'Hardly,' I thought.

Accept the honour. That was in the imperative.

Somewhat shocked, I bowed in turn. I was rather tempted to salute.

Of Raphael, he said, referring to my church.

Yes, I replied.

Then shall you heal! he pronounced. My head spun slightly as it received an electric shock-type slap of salmon-pink and golden tingles. I had to totter off to the shop to calm down with a bit of retail distraction.

I bought the Gudula lantern, just like last time—no, not at all like last time; this time, I wasn't afraid. However, pottering around the shop didn't dissolve what was, in effect, a call to worship channelled from the angel of Michael. I was being summoned through every cell of my being and not even the god of Mammon residing in the Cathedral shop had a faraday cage strong enough to dilute it, especially when there is also a guardian angel figuratively jumping up and down and slapping you over the head with map-of-Brussels tea towel.

Eventually, I surrendered. Spiritual surrender is not so much about giving in and submitting to what isn't really wanted as finding the core discipline and strength to step up and do what is asked. It's not soft or soppy at all. Ask Jonah.

With a sigh, I made my way to the High Altar. These are the places where Mass used to take place with the priest standing with his back to the congregation and everyone forming a vortex for the incoming Glory. Nowadays, the priest faces the people, further down the church in what is essentially a dumbing-down of the whole process. Not surprising that if you take even unacknowledged mystical truths away that the congregation also leaves. Yes, I know people used to go to church because they had to, not because they wanted to, but the one percent who wanted to go *could* login to the mystical aspect and that was enough to ensure that the sun still rose and the glaciers didn't melt.

Yes, that last sentence shocked me too. It came into my head the moment I sat down in the chapel itself, before I had even had time to think about whether I was going to kneel, fold my hands or say a prayer or blessing.

'The fall of Christianity is what's causing global warming?' I thought.

No. The fall of humanity is causing global warming. The loss of faith and the rise of greed. You all consider 'my life' and 'I want' more important than 'the life' and 'we all need.'; Humanity has to remember 'I AM Life' to heal its Mother… and itself.

Just as I was digesting that massive concept, I sensed a kind of recalibrative susurration. Angels don't get cross or frustrated as such but they do have to re-focus when we humans divert them. They're essentially like SatNavs and, in the same way, any irritation you perceive when the machinery says 'recalculating' is actually your own guilty projection. In this case, the angel was re-routing back to the subject that needed to be addressed.

I settled down and cleared my mind. Not easy for any of us but essential if what is being communicated is not going to be blocked or avoided. I'd only got the global warning message because it caught me by surprise.

Okay… it was all about using St. Raphael's as a vortex of healing. Not about me (phew). I wasn't to become a kind of John of God, the controversial Brazilian healer, but I was the doorkeeper of the church and, yes, I would be able to carry some of the healing energies on parish visits.

'One condition,' I said.

You would set conditions? On Grace?

'Yes. That no one realises that I have anything to do with it.'

That is how it is. What is your condition? Angels don't express surprise and they don't understand our egos but that was still a relief. I know you might be thinking that it might be rather nice to be known as a great healer but, trust me, the road to misery and corruption is paved with good egoic intentions. Jesus' temptation in the desert—the one with turning stones into bread—sounds so sensible, doesn't it? Feed everyone; be the hero! But once you start feeding that fish instead of teaching people how to fish (to mix metaphors), you will become the guru and the demands will increase to the point that you're run ragged and nobody is learning anything. No thanks! My life is complicated enough as it is.

'I set no conditions,' I said.

Good.

We sat in silence then. The angel had made its communication and no more was required. I was quietly boggling at what might actually transpire and aware that if St. Raphael's did become a centre of healing it would impinge on my life quite a bit.

If I was still there.

Chapter Twenty-One

I STAYED IN Brussels for five days, pottering, eating a lot of cheese and even more gaufres (but not necessarily together). After a couple of days, I was becoming really rather relaxed as it was clear that my universe didn't seem to have any plans to slip over into the other part-Bruxellian parallel world or throw me into another court hearing. I'd been prepared to try and deal with that if it happened but very relieved that it hadn't. In fact, I had two really rather lovely weeks of holiday, during which I wandered around Europe on foot and by train. I wasn't lonely because I had a ghost hound, a guardian angel and a selection of church angels to keep me company. None of them were terribly good conversationalists but that suited me just fine. Seraphim drifted in and out of my world; I expect she had other things to do but she was always curled up by my side every morning when I woke and she still liked to dry my legs after a bath or shower.

I went to Bruges and Lille and then, finally, submitted to that strange calling I'd felt in that parallel universe—to go to Paris for a few days. For some reason I knew that I needed to go. Once there, I hedged my bets by treating myself to a smart Parisian suit as a kind of self-defence action. Just because I had been honoured with the title of 'priestess' didn't mean I would keep my position or my church. As I lived in my own home, next to St. Raphael's, I could still be the priestess of the healing angels there whether or not I officiated. They could hardly ban me from the building (or could they?!). So, I passed a little time considering my alternatives if I was asked to leave. I could become an independent—a 'hedge priest' and a celebrant—someone who officiates at weddings, baby-namings and funerals outside of sacred space. Apparently such folk earn quite a lot of money nowadays and I now had a suitable—and rather elegant—outfit in which to do it. Basically,

I was incredibly lucky that I lived in a world where I would most probably be okay financially—apart from the sense of loss of a specific vocation. And I knew, too, that my vocation itself could never truly be touched by the decisions of another. I had written a book that sold relatively well in Church circles and had, so far, resisted any attempt to write a follow-up, despite requests from the publishers. I'd told them I had nothing more to say but I suspected that the calls of unemployment might bring a little inspiration…

On my last day in Paris, Seraphim seemed keen to lead me along the banks of the Seine next to the Champs Elysées. We ended up at the Chapelle Expiatoire, or 'Chapel of Atonement' set in its own small and pretty gardens containing just one yew tree, oddly still redolent with scarlet arils.

I didn't need Seraphim or Hero to tell me to stop there; something told me that this was the place I needed to be.

I sat on the steps of this beautiful chapel watching Seraphim wandering in its garden, sniffing ghostly smells (I have no idea how that works so don't ask). After a while, she started digging at the base of the yew. Instinct made me try to stop her—dear God, how much trouble would I be in with a dog that damaged a park space? But, of course, she was only digging in the ghostly world.

What was odder was that another dog joined her—another ghost dog. This one seemed to be some kind of spaniel.

Thisbe, whispered Hero but that didn't mean anything to me. I presumed it was the spaniel's name.

I watched them cautiously, remembering some of my research on yews. There was a book written in 1664 by a botanist, Robert Turner, that claimed decaying corpses in graveyards released poisonous gases which were absorbed by yews. He claimed this was why the tree was so poisonous. The ancient Greek physician Galen of Pergamon even claimed lying under a yew could kill you.

Another legend said that yews were planted in graveyards because the roots were believed to grow through the eyes of the dead to hold them in place. Thanks to mobile data, I was able to look up 'burials at the Chapelle Expiatoire' discovering that many of the folk who were executed in the French revolution were buried exactly here, including Marie Antoinette. Google revealed that she had a spaniel called Thisbe. I realised I was holding my breath.

I watched, frozen to the steps as Seraphim and Thisbe dug up the etheric remains of the martyred French Queen.

Marie Antoinette's physical body was moved many years later and now rests in the Cathedral Saint-Denis but her ghost was here, tied to the ground for centuries. Why? Because there was something else there too, revealed by those powerful claws scrabbling in the earth; a dark energy tied up with her and three of her children who, I found out later, were called Louis-Charles, Louis-Joseph and a baby, Sophie.

They were wrapped in a demon's energy, and had been trapped underground, lost and despairing. Seraphim's and Thisbe's digging revealed all four and my spirit sight winced at the spiral of pain I could only begin to perceive. Slowly a cloud of darkness emerged through the soil. The stench was enough to make me retch.

I know (because I'm that kind of annoying person) that Marie Antoinette was more sinned against than sinning, that she never said 'let them eat cake' and that three of her four children had died very young but I'd never really considered the kind of emotional pain she must have experienced in a short life of unbearable loneliness and tragedy. It made sense that demons had been part of the French Revolution—probably Archons—and it seemed that whatever this particular darkness was, it had managed to hide the tragic queen and her dead children from any spirit rescue attempt.

It was vile; oozing and hungry, reaching into the four ghosts like chains of maggots. They still existed, just, but the damage was immense. I had no idea what to do.

The darkness turned what was left of a face towards the dogs and licked what might once have been lips.

'*Seraphim, Thisbe, à moi!*' I commanded, without thinking. '*Derrière moi!*' They obeyed, just escaping a kind of grey fog that exuded from whatever it was that ate life. But then, of course, it observed me.

I was aware that I was, for the moment, stronger than it. It had been starving for a very long time but it had enough strength to attempt some kind of attack and the moment it could eat it would regain strength in seconds. And I was good meat; fully living and not exactly slim. It could dine out on me for decades. And as I could perceive it, it knew I was within its world and fair game.

I couldn't risk love; I just couldn't. I couldn't walk forward into it and just love it because I was alone and it was unlovable and I was afraid. You can't be afraid and love simultaneously. But I could say an exorcism and I could call for help. I had a protective angel, after all!

'Rus-el!' I hissed, to call that crimson-and-scarlet spirit down from the heavens and he came, a magnificent warrior, armed and ready to defend.

It ate him. Of course it did. He deflated like a balloon while simultaneously going 'pop.' I'm going to have to re-name that angel Kenny.

Worse, eating an angel strengthened the darkness. I started chanting the Latin exorcism, looking around for something with which I could make a cross. Useless. It crept towards me, wary and sending out questing tendrils of slime to attempt to taste me. Hero braced herself, wrapping her wings around me and then she was gone. Seraphim kissed my hand and was gone too. A small part of me wailed; an echo of Marie Antoinette's despair touched my heart and soul as I was abandoned.

I won't describe the feeling of a soul-eater licking and tasting its intended victim; I still have nightmares about it and you simply don't want to know. All I knew, myself, is that I could hear myself screaming without even being aware that my vocal chords were working.

The grease and slime began to nibble at my hands, pointlessly held out to ward it off. It wasn't in any hurry; the more I screamed as it began to eat, the greater the fun. I felt myself becoming wrapped in a dark sticky spider's web of spikes.

Then the howling began. It grew louder. And louder. It was a call, a plea, a cry. And within a minute, its cadence changed to the belling of a pack, a huge pack and dozens—no, hundreds—ghost dogs thundered down from the sky. Seraphim was leading them,

Thisbe was there and so was Margot. Hero too. Marcus's children were racing to save me.

It was a Charge of the Light Brigade at first; a terrible, losing fight and my heart broke as the demon caught hold of the leader, my beautiful ghost hound. She screamed as it snatched at her and began to eat and I screamed too, running forward and hitting out at the demon like a helpless child. Touching it was like falling through ice into paralysingly cold water and I froze like a statue while other dogs leapt past me, tearing and biting. Eventually, I was able to move again as the sheer volume of dogs began to have an effect. Yes, the demon grew slightly stronger with each one it ate but more and more and more poured out of the skies to attack it, each one offering its soul to save one puny little human being; well five puny human beings even if four of them were barely even ghosts. Okay, okay, Dog *is* God written backwards.

Eventually, they held it at bay. Enough dogs had torn at it to destabilise it seriously but it still lived (if you can call it that) and there was stasis. In an attempt to weaken me, for the dogs were all spiritually attached to me, it spat out the remains of my beautiful ghost hound.

I ran to her and cradled her in my arms. My beloved girl… I bent my head over her torn and mangled body and wept, my stupidly beautiful tears falling all over her.

And I loved… for grief is the price of love and cannot be separated from it.

Seraphim's dark brown eyes opened and she tried to lick me from her shattered mouth. And a shaft of light shot from her body down a dim, cloudy chord, still linking her to the demon. My love for her, somehow, in an extraordinary miracle of Grace, connected into the loving grief of every living human being who had ever lost a dog. It was a river of sorrow that became an arrow of fire. I felt it, and the wonder and power of it, this powerhouse of passionate love that channelled itself through me and my poor little ghost hound and into that shadow of darkness and hate.

For one moment I felt its own, eternal, despair at its perceived separation from all that was good and loving. And then it collapsed into itself in its own kind of surrender. In love, it died and dissolved. I don't know where, if anywhere, it went but nothing remained. There was no fairy-like spirit as there had been for the Archon. For a moment, there was a stillness and then the yew tree groaned and slowly, terribly, it fell. One smallish branch hit me, knocking me unconscious and dislocating my left shoulder which, conveniently, explained to the people already racing to the scene why this British tourist had been screaming blue murder, right next to the Champs Elysées.

Yes, I woke up in hospital. That's been a bit of a theme, hasn't it?... I think I started crying almost as soon as I recovered consciousness. They thought it was part of the concussion but I was weeping for my ghost hound as well as for shock and retrospective terror. This time, there was no Alessina sitting peacefully by my bed and although my French is tolerable it took a while to understand '*votre épaule a été disloquée et vous avez une commotion cérébrale*' and there was no one to whom I could possibly explain my pain. Later, I came to appreciate the phrase 'un commotion cérébrale.' It seemed most appropriate.

I'd not been unconscious long; it was still the same day, approaching evening. All I could do was lie there in the Parisian hospital bed and wait for night in the hope that Jon might come...

Marcus came first. Or, rather, Thisbe came first. She jumped up on my bed, followed by a group of mixed-breed ghost dogs. Then Marcus walked through the door, just like a real human being. This time he appeared to be wearing scrubs so I didn't recognise him at first but he sat on my bed and took my right hand in his ghostly one. We didn't actually speak for a long time—apart from anything else, I was on a ward full of people and talking to myself out loud would have set off a few alarms—but we communicated all the same. He told me, somehow, that the ghost dogs who were destroyed were *only* destroyed from one incarnation and that their souls, kept safe in the great soul of Dog, still existed. They could never manifest again as that particular dog but they could still present themselves from another life on Earth. Yes, I know, it's complicated but it was also comforting. It was probably also ineffable.

'Seraphim?' I asked, with more tears falling. I seemingly

couldn't stop them at the moment; it was probably the commotion cérébrale. 'She is now *Destiny*,' said Marcus. 'Her colouring is different and she may not recognise you, but she still *is*.'

'Can I see her?'

Marcus smiled and waved an arm. A tricolour ghost hound appeared by his feet and stood on her hind legs, with her paws on his knees. I could see her clearly as, at Marcus's bidding, she turned to look at me.

'Hello Destiny,' I squeaked through tears and she reached out her nose towards me. Her eyes were a lighter colour and her nose longer but there were similarities. She eased herself up on the bed and bumped noses with me in greeting and then curled up on the bed with her head on my legs.

'Well, as I live and breathe,' said Marcus, who clearly did neither. 'There is a remembering. You have known each other in another life. This is good.'

It was good. Yes, I know; I'm still not comfortable with this recurring idea of 'other lives' but then, what do I know? Seeing that slightly different hound did ease the pain somehow. She wasn't Seraphim and yet, strangely, she was.

We talked, Marcus and I (or rather thought-communicated) until Jon arrived. I can't tell you all that we said but it was loving. And yes, I knew now that somewhere, sometime, our lives had been linked before and that we knew each other. And that we would meet again. Once Jon was here, Marcus politely left and Destiny left with him. I cried again because I was so relieved that Jon knew to come given that I was on 'holiday' and… well, just because.

He, too, sat on my bed and held my hand. He told me of a great cycle of life where the souls of Marie Antoinette and her children had been held back from the heavens through the grief, hatred and despair of their times and how Seraphim, in one incarnation, had been one of their hounds. That she had come to me primarily to help her former loves to find their way to the heavens.

'How did she know? How did it happen?' I wanted to know—the 'cursèd hows' as Jon calls them. All he would say is that the Universe works in patterns; Divine Order, he called it. We play our parts in those patterns and they work for us and in us according to our level of acceptance of spirit. If we believe in miracles, it is easier to experience them; if we will give up ('give UP') our resistance, we can become an active part of a positive flow.

'You had a near-death experience, Bel,' he said. 'Your brain is wired differently from most people's. You can see a wider picture and you *know* that love is the answer to everything. And you know that most of the world can't handle that knowledge. Your job—and you *have* chosen to accept it!—is to hold the faith.

'One thing I will tell you and it will blow what little brain you have left, after repeated bangs on the head.'

'Oh thanks!'

'It's all happening *now* in the heavens. Linear time only exists in the lower worlds. So things can be changed and adjusted *at any time* with full consciousness. Marie Antoinette and her children's hell did not last three hundred years because Thisbe and Seraphim brought you in contemporary time. She is now recovering well and can move on. The time scale is irrelevant.'

'But Seraphim was destroyed.' Another tear.

'Yes, Seraphim *was* destroyed but the soul that became Seraphim could never be destroyed and, because of who you've become, you could experience her from another incarnation.'

'It's a lot to take in, Jon.'

'It is. That's why most folk don't know; because they wouldn't *want* to understand. And, frankly, if everyone knew that it all worked out in the heavens, there would be a lot more people taking themselves there early and missing out on the lessons of life.'

'Some of the lessons of life are incalculably hard.'

'They are but I'll tell you another secret. We *all* go through all the stages of life. Before we're done, we are all murderers, all murdered, all disabled, all full-bodied, all straight, all gay and so on and so on. We are here to experience it all so we stop judging it all and learn to love.'

'Really?'

'Really.'

'Oh.'

Chapter Twenty-Two

Oh how much I love coming home! My little stone cottage is a haven of beauty and the village itself is a delight. Yes, there is the obligatory Facebook group where people mostly complain about dog mess and bad parking but rural Devon is still a wonderful place to live, even if you are slightly brown.

After I was released from hospital, had managed to explain to my hotel, paid up and got my luggage back, I took the Eurostar back to the UK and got home at about ten PM. Lucie picked me up from the station after I texted her the time my train got into Okehampton. *I'm lesbian the horse at 9.30* she texted back. I can only assume she meant 'leaving the house.' I managed to shake her off at the doorstep with a hug, genuine thanks and a packet of Parisian macaroons and resisted opening the scary letter from the diocesan office that was waiting for me until the following morning.

The kitchen ceiling had been repaired, probably because the insurance company didn't want any more diatribes from Mrs Tiggy who had loyally (and justifiably, according to Robbie) picked up the mantle of sorting it out. She had watched the repair folk like a hawk and reported that they had done the work in double-quick time. The woman is a powerhouse and I am oh, so grateful that she is—mostly—on my side. Both she and Lucie had left me supplies to come home to so I could eat like a Quing. Quing is one of my favourite words at the moment as we are still not entirely used to having a King in the UK rather than a Queen. It's suitably non-binary for the modern world, don't you think?

That night, Jon and I watched the birth of a star on the edge of our galaxy and talked over my Earthly options before going on to work with Sam and Callista at yet another hospice without a chapel-vortex for the dead. Afterwards, we took a detour to the hospital regions of the afterlife. I'd been there before to visit my late fiancé, Paul, but I hadn't realised the depth of the work that was done here. Ward after ward of recovering dead people… It's hard to imagine but, I guess, if you die of a long and terrible illness, your etheric takes a while to let go of time and therefore has to take some in order to recover; it's not necessarily instant that you are dancing and singing again. We saw cancer patients, glowing with hope and relief as they saw etheric amputated limbs and breasts re-growing healthily, suicides who had lived so long in despair that they needed help to slough off the remaining feelings of hopelessness (and sometimes the temporary utter horror that death did not mean eternal nothingness, too). We saw folk from the Ukraine and other war-torn areas as their etheric bodies rebuilt themselves. *This* was the kind of hospital I liked; everyone came out of here well. Jon took me to one dark room with a restless, half-awake man in it. He was attended by a team of loving Jewish folk—you could tell their faith by the men's yarmulkes and the women's headscarves. He woke briefly while we watched and his horror and shame were difficult to observe. He obviously hated himself with a vengeance.

'He's been here in pretty much real time since 1945,' said Jon and then I understood; the man was being cared-for by the very people he had murdered in a concentration camp.

'This, for him, is hell,' said Jon. 'To realise that those he thought inhuman are deeply human, more loving and more capable than he ever was. He is realising the depth of his cruelty and thoughtlessness and he is having to realise it with the very people he killed.'

'And they have forgiven him?'

'Yes. For some, of course, it takes a while but most of what you call "victims" can truly let go and let God once they are here. If they can't then they remain here until they can. It's not bad in the hospital regions; many patients have their own rooms and their own gardens and pets. But no one leaves until they are willing to think anew. You can't rise up with the heavy energy of hatred. And the true test that you have let go and moved on is that you would be willing to care for the very perpetrator of your life's tragedy.'

'I can't see most people on Earth liking that!'

'No. "An eye for an eye" and all that. But it works as a system. It heals.'

I could see that but even for someone like me who teaches forgiveness and works in the heavens, I could see how hard it might be to understand that this is how God works.

'Hell only exists in our thoughts and beliefs,' I said.

'Exactly, said Jon.

We were here to visit one particular room where four souls were residing, having their etheric and spirit aspects re-woven into healing. Marie Antoinette and her children. And Seraphim.

My beautiful ghost hound, in her new-to-me colours, was playing with Thisbe and the children on the floor of the room. Now I could see how she had been Louis-Joseph's dog, beloved of all the family and, when they hadn't come home to the heavens to find her, she had missed them enough to find her way to a human who could trace them. It had taken time and tragedy but Destiny—or Destinée as they called her—had persevered. She, even more than Thisbe, had loved them with all her heart.

'*Merci, merci beaucoup Madame!*' said the former queen, a rather weak-faced young woman, still pale and scarred from being chewed on by a demon and from trying to protect her children. '*Je vous remercie. Je peux à peine y croire. C'est un miracle.*' She tried to jump up from her bed and staggered—she was still etherically in heavy eighteenth century clothing for some reason, rather than the simple shift in which she would have gone to her death. Jon caught her and helped her to stand up and she extended one rather regal hand out for me to kiss.

'*Je vous en prie, votre majestée,*' I replied, bending over the hand and trying not to giggle at the ridiculousness of it all. If I really wanted to shoot myself in the foot at any future disciplinary or mental health hearing, all I would have to do would be to say 'I met Marie Antoinette last night' and I'd be heading for a straitjacket.

Destiny thumped the end of her tail gently on the floor in a slightly apologetic way.

I felt incredibly sad; I had learnt to love my ghost hound but this wasn't really her and I knew this version of her must stay in the heavens with her own family. My legs would remain eternally un-dried by her tongue.

'Was it you who sent me the yew arils?' I asked her, but of course she couldn't answer.

'*Les arilles d'if?*' said Jon to the former Queen. She laughed. '*La danse de l'if de grand-père!*' she replied. '*c'était une légende dans notre famille. Chaque fois que nous voyions un if, nous demandions "qui est là-dedans?" Et on porte des arilles d'ifs quand on joue à cache-cache.*'

'They played hide and seek with yew arils as part of the game,' said Jon to me. 'Something to do with the Queen's grandfather-in-law and a Yew Ball. So there's certainly some connection but I'm not sure of the details.'

I found out later that the Yew Ball at Versailles was held in February 1745, to mark the marriage of the Dauphin to Maria Teresa Rafaela of Spain. Apparently, Louis XVI and some of his courtiers had dressed up as yew trees to disguise themselves while the king searched for the woman who was to become his favourite, Madame de Pompadour. Exactly how all this tied up was beyond me but some ineffable pattern of ghost dogs, guardians and magic had conspired to make some strange British vicar in the twenty-first century become obsessed enough with yew arils and a ghost hound to go and look for four lost souls hidden under a tree.

'All things work together for good, to those who love God,' wrote St Paul but I think that one takes the (chocolate) biscuit…

After taking our leave, we repaired to the country-house-in-the-sky scenario where I first met my two discarnate friends, Sam and Callista, and had a few heavenly drinks. They wanted all the details about love and the demons—and yew trees and strange French Queens—and, in return, I learnt a little about their lives. Sam died in a car accident at the age of 58 and Callista at 97 'of rampant old age,' as she put it. Neither had lived to see the twenty-first century and neither was exactly upset about that. It was lovely to spend a little more time getting to know them better.

'So, the arils…' I said, eventually. 'Was that all about Marie Antoinette? And is it over?'

'They were messages to draw you to that particular chapel in Paris,' said Sam. 'Without them, would you ever have gone there?'

'I don't know. It was a long and complicated path but I suppose if there hadn't been any in the jam, I wouldn't have noticed the one at the Bishop's palace; I wouldn't have jumped on him and...' I paused. Without that weird and horrible experience, Judith might not be pregnant but that seemed a really complicated way to achieve a miracle.

'I just don't know. I probably wouldn't have taken a holiday; I wouldn't have been in Europe and if I *had*, I wouldn't have been so observant about the yew tree. One of the things I can't understand is why *that* yew didn't act as a portal—that seems to be what they can do, after all. And another thing I don't understand is why no one had located Marie Antoinette and her children before.'

'We screwed up,' said Sam. 'I could tell you that we don't have the staff; that she and her children were hidden very well but, basically, we screwed up. Thank you, Bel. You got through.'

I waved a hand dismissively. Easy to do when it's all over (for the moment at least) and you are drinking the finest (if probably imaginary) champagne. 'But are there others?' That, I really wanted to know.

'Almost certainly,' said Callista, sadly. 'All we can do is our best. And thank God that we can retrieve them in contemporary time whether or not it takes us centuries to get there.'

'The thing is...' said Jon, who was enjoying a pint of Ma Batham's Mild from the Black Country of the 1970s '...the thing is, life isn't like fiction. It doesn't have to make sense; it doesn't have to tie up all the loose ends; it just goes on fitting bits together or not.'

We all nodded wisely. 'And it's ineffable,' we chorused, raising our glasses to each other.

I woke up to the sound of Mrs Tiggy clambering up the stairs with a cup of tea. She scolded me for not washing up my supper ('what did your last slave die of?'), for leaving dirty laundry on the floor by the washing machine and for not opening my post, pointedly handing me the diocesan letter.

'Go on, Amabel. Get it over with.'

So I did.

The letter was from the brand new Dean. I'd not registered that any such person had actually arrived. So far, so bad.

But then it got better. The Very Reverend Alexander Dubois wrote that he hoped I had had a good and relaxing holiday and that he was pleased to inform me that his Grace the bishop had also benefited from a short holiday and was 'feeling much more like himself again.'

Intriguing. Very.

The Dean went on to ask if I could call on him at the earliest convenient opportunity so that we could become acquainted and discuss a few matters. Perhaps I could email him with a suitable time.

Oh shit.

Still, it could have been a lot worse. This sounded like a possible disciplinary rather than a court case—and what had happened to the bishop? Had the new Dean spotted something? Was he an exorcist? That would be a turn up for the books if so.

Taking the bit between my teeth I emailed, suggesting we meet that very afternoon to get it over with, whatever it was. The reply, within half an hour, courteously suggested the following day at three PM and I felt an absolute prat for assuming I was so important that the Dean would drop everything just to see me.

The day was taken up with washing, sorting stuff, Lucie's totally valid concerns about the sanity of the Parish Council and slightly breathless announcement that she and Will had been out for supper and to the cinema… and wandering down to the village shop for a bottle of red and some chocolate. On the way, I saw Judith Monroe looking radiant. She confided in me that she had had her first ultrasound and so far, things were going well. Obviously she wasn't telling anyone until the twelve weeks 'safe point', but given her palpable joy I expect a lot of people could guess.

And I saw Micki, just a few seconds before I saw Sharon and her daughter Félicie walking up the lane that counts as our High Street, ahead of me. He was looking really well, off the lead and trotting beside Félicie.

I greeted them: 'Hello Sharon, hello Félicie, hello Micki! How are you today?'

Oh boy, had I got my tone wrong! Sharon and Félicie turned round and their faces were grim; Félicie had clearly been crying.

'What did you say?' said Sharon. Félicie just stared at the ground. Micki put his paws up on her thighs and tried to lick her hands. Damn, damn, damn. He was a ghost dog. Now I was concentrating, I could see that. Oh God, had I hurt them more?

'Micki?' I said, as a question, already knowing the answer.

'Yesterday,' said Sharon. 'We had to call the vet round. We were all there.'

'Oh I am so very sorry.' I put a hand out to touch her shoulder, giving her the choice whether to step forward into the touch or avoid it. She stepped forward and then leant in for a hug.

'Félicie keeps asking if they go to heaven,' she said softly, into my shoulder, her voice shaking. 'I don't know what to say.'

I squeezed her tight and then let go and crouched down to the eight-year-old. Micki started to dance in the street, going round and round in circles, chasing his tail.

'Félicie, dogs do go to heaven,' I said. 'I *know* they do. And they come back to see the people they love too. Micki is here now and he's turning in anti-clockwise circles, chasing his tail. He wants you to know that he loves you and that he feels well and happy. He looks young again.'

It was a huge gamble. Sharon looked at me as if I were mad but Félicie's eyes were almost circular.

'*Really?*' she breathed. 'Where is he?'

I put my hand out to Micki and he came over to sniff it. I tickled him under his chin and said, 'he's here. His head is in my hand. Can you see if you can feel him? It will be very faint but he will try his hardest to let you sense that he is here.

Félicie put one hand right through Micki, who shied back; I dread to think what it feels like, as a ghost to have a human poke you.

'I can't feel anything,' she said. 'Why can *you* see him if I can't? I'm the one who loved him!'

'Well, that's a very good question,' I said. 'But first let's see what we can do to help you feel him, shall we?'

Still crouched down, I took her hand and laid it where Micki's back was/might have been and he stood quietly, perceiving what I was trying to do.

'Close your eyes,' I said, thanking God there was no traffic passing and very few pedestrians about. 'Let your fingers feel, very gently.' *Please God!* I prayed and, to be honest, I never knew if that prayer was for her to experience her beloved dog or for me not to be totally humiliated. Probably a bit of both.

Félicie mimed stroking Micki. She knew his shape well from memory and the little dog moved with her hand to encourage what contact could be made.

'I… I think so,' she said. And, sitting down in the middle of the road, burst into tears.

I looked up at Sharon to apologise but she was standing very still and staring down at the little dog. Quite some woman is Sharon!

'I think I see something,' she said, quietly.

Micki put his paws on Félicie's chest and licked her face.

'That tickles!' she said and laughed through the tears.

'Reverend Amabel!' called a voice. Drat, it was Sandra Collingwood. I stood up and put a welcoming smile on my face. 'Sandra!' and the moment was gone. Both Sharon and Félicie blinked. The world turned again and went back to what passed for normal. I endured Sandra's litany of complaints about life for five minutes while Sharon and her daughter went to the post office and, managing to break away without causing visible offence, turned to go back home.

Something made me turn to look back and I saw what I thought was Marcus, dressed like an average twenty-first century man in jeans and fleece. He was waiting for Micki. Both Sharon and Félicie were standing on the post office steps staring at the space where he stood.

There might have to be some discussion another time but I was prepared for that. As far as I was concerned, the more pet-owners knew the truth the better. And to the nether regions with Bishops, Deans and whoever.

By 2.45 PM the next day I was in Exeter, parking the car and checking my hair and make-up. I was wearing a skirt and a matching clerical shirt and looking as respectable as possible. Waves of love from Lucie, Alessina and Robbie surrounded me and Mrs Tiggy had lent me one of her beautifully-ironed cotton hankies 'just in case.'

I'm glad she did.

The Dean didn't keep me waiting long though those few minutes were agony. At last his PA, Jennifer, waved me in with a smile and I opened the door to his office.

I had a vague impression of a grey haired man with a strong face and dark eyebrows, wearing a blue clerical shirt, rising up from his chair to come around his desk and shake my hand. But it was only an impression. I didn't even look at him. I was too busy staring at Margot.

Bella's adventures will continue in *Some Velvet Morning*.